Marcel Swofis
Amsterdam
28 nov 2008

Memoirs of the
Life of Monsieur
de Voltaire
Written by Himself

Voltaire

Translated by Andrew Brown

ET REMOTISSIMA PROPE

Hesperus Classics

Hesperus Classics

Published by Hesperus Press Limited

4 Rickett Street, London sw6 1ru

www.hesperuspress.com

First published in 1784

First published by Hesperus Press Limited, 2007

Introduction and English language translation © Andrew Brown, 2007

Foreword © Ruth Scurr, 2007

Designed and typeset by Fraser Muggeridge studio

Printed in Jordan by Jordan National Press

isbn: 1-84391-152-3

isbn13: 978-1-84391-152-4

CONTENTS

FOREWORD

None of us knows which, in retrospect, are the best years of our lives. The time of deepest happiness, greatest achievement, or most passionate love may not always announce itself in passing. And even when one suspects the best has been and gone, it is hard to stop hoping better will come.

In Voltaire's life, 1759 was pivotal: the year he published *Candide* (or *Optimism*) and spread throughout Europe a humane challenge to the enormity of human suffering: 'Appalled, stupefied, distraught, covered in blood and shaking uncontrollably, Candide said to himself: "If this is the best of all possible worlds, what must the others be like?"'*

Candide was an instant best-seller, adding to Voltaire's already considerable wealth. Aged sixty-five, worth about a million *livres*, he was living outside Geneva on estates he had purchased at Ferney and Tourney. In his *Memoirs*, composed around this time, he boasts, 'I have so arranged my destiny that I am now independent both in Switzerland, on the territory of Geneva, and in France. I hear a lot of talk about freedom, but I do not think there has ever been an individual in Europe who has procured himself such freedom as mine.'

Free as he felt himself, Voltaire looked back with bitterness on the constraints he had had to overcome. The 'shitbags of literature' for a start: those who had libelled and defamed him because they were envious when his plays and poems succeeded. Since childhood, he was set on a literary career, but categorically dismissed the delusion that it might prove a means to freedom as well as an expression of it. 'I have always preferred liberty above everything else. Few writers can say the same. Most of them are poor; poverty wears down one's courage; and every philosopher at Court becomes as much of a slave as the first officer of the Crown.'

Despite himself, he found power seductive. 'Everyone knows that you have to suffer indignities from kings', he wrote, but his intimate relationship with royalty was consensual. Frederick of Prussia sent flattering letters to Voltaire, who obtained permission from Louis XV of France for an extended visit to Berlin. Poetry and philosophy were common ground between Frederick and Voltaire. They fell out when someone spread the rumour that the latter thought the former's poetry no good. The rumour was true and in his memoirs Voltaire makes relentless fun of Frederick's feeble versification. Afterwards, in retreat near Geneva, he was delighted to discover 'what kings never give, or rather what they deprive one of: peace and liberty'. And yet, he cannot resist mentioning that since he acquired tranquillity, far from court, Frederick has begun communicating again, sending yet more poetry, an opera that is 'the worst thing he has done'.

Love was another constraint. Voltaire's brilliant companion, the scientist and scholar Emilie du Châtelet, died in childbirth in her early forties. The child was neither her husband's nor Voltaire's. All concerned were grief stricken. While she was still alive, Voltaire claims, he told Frederick that 'philosopher for philosopher, I prefer a lady to a king', but after her death there was nothing to keep him from Prussia. Following the deterioration in his relations with Frederick, Voltaire found 'the consolation of my life' in his niece, Mme Denis. She was with him as he contentedly composed his memoirs: 'While I was in my retreat enjoying the sweetest life imaginable, I had the small philosophical pleasure of seeing that the kings of Europe were not able to enjoy this same happy tranquillity, and of concluding that the situation of a private individual is often preferable to that of the greatest monarchs.'

Voltaire professed himself so happy he was almost ashamed, gazing out from a private idyll at war-torn Europe, ruined and drenched in blood. In May 1759, he received yet another unwelcome poem from Frederick, insulting the king of France. Dragged against his will back into politics, he informed the French authorities, who arranged for a counter poem to be composed, insulting the King of Prussia. Voltaire played amusedly with the idea of these two absurd poems becoming the foundations of European peace. Then invoked Corneille: 'This, my lovely Emilie, is the point we have reached.'

The quote is poignant with Voltaire's own Emilie ten years dead. It was, he noted, somewhat ridiculous 'to talk about myself to myself': he was starting to feel lonely. The memoirs are sanguine – sometimes joyous – in tone, but they carry an undercurrent of something far worse than reckoning past mistakes or insults, even when the bitterness they caused still lingers. It is the simple passage of time. There was much still ahead of Voltaire. He died in 1778, having composed (or perhaps dictated) in his last few years another autobiographical fragment (*Commentaire historique sur les œuvres de l'auteur de la Henriade*). By the end of his life his grief for Emilie and his disappointment in Frederick had tempered, even if his irritation at the 'rascality of literature' never diminished. By contrast, the earlier memoirs are raw. In 1759 Voltaire was still close to the defining events of his public and private life. He had found refuge in Mme Denis and their estates outside Geneva. He was about to throw himself into improving the lives of his villagers and publicly campaigning against infamy. There is no reason to think he protested too much when he proclaimed the almost embarrassing extent of his private happiness. And yet there are hints in the memoirs that he already knew the high tide of his passion had passed. He would never again fall prey to 'utter devastation' at the death of a woman he loved, or fail to resist the flattery of 'a king who was also a poet, musician and philosopher, and who claimed to love me'. The memoirs of 1759 are precious above all for showing us how Voltaire saw his life when he was at its imaginative centre: on the cusp between living expectantly and recollecting in tranquillity.

– Ruth Scurr, 2007

* *Candide, or Optimism*, translated and edited by Theo Cuffe (London: Penguin, 2005).

INTRODUCTION

'A scandalous libel', Carlyle called it. The dyspeptic Sage of Chelsea had no great admiration for Voltaire's *Memoirs*, since the person they (in his view) libelled, Frederick the Great, was not only a personal hero of his, but the man over whose biography he laboured (plagued by more than occasional doubts as to whether the Prussian King was entirely worth such devotion) between 1851 and 1865. Instead of taking Voltaire's comparatively brief and improvised work as a contribution to our understanding of Voltaire, Carlyle read it as essentially being about Frederick. And as such, it was a complete travesty of the facts, written by Voltaire in 'a kind of fury' as an act of revenge on a king who had first courted and then humiliated him; a work filled with 'wild exaggerations and perversions, or even downright lies', one which imputed to Frederick 'all crimes... natural and unnatural', and was, in its frenzy, like a 'Devil's Head, done in phosphorus on the walls of the black-hole' by an artist locked up, with justice, as a madman.

While the *Memoirs* do not quite live up (or down) to the blistering anti-hype of this splenetic bluster, they are certainly one of Voltaire's most fascinating, and yet lesser-known, works. That we can read them at all is fortuitous. Voltaire seems to have composed them in conditions of relative secrecy: he may have intended them for only posthumous publication. Their asperity of tone, mocking disrespect for the Establishment (or those of its members who had happened to offend Voltaire), indiscreet gossip about eminent personages, and *saeva indignatio* at the persistence of *l'infâme*, might well have made publication too dangerous while their author was still alive and (despite his fame and his prudent residence just the other side of the French border) still subject to the caprice of monarchs and the rage of prelates. Some scholars say that he burnt the original of the *Memoirs*, but made at least one copy (which was then, to his chagrin, stolen). But this was a man who seems to have wanted everything he ever wrote (and a great deal of what he said) to be, sooner or later, in the public domain. At all events, his niece, Mme Denis, inherited his papers on his death, and two copies of the *Memoirs* were found among them. One ended up in St Petersburg, as part of the library of Catherine the Great (who at one stage showed an interest in having Voltaire's entire oeuvre published in her capital city); the other was purchased by Beaumarchais, who had rented an old fort at Kehl, on the Rhine, and set about publishing (on twenty-four printing presses) the first *Complete Works*, in which the *Memoirs* were the last volume.

The *Memoirs* had probably been written in 1758–9, making them contemporary with *Candide*. In their almost ferocious gaiety, with sporadic moments of anger and an underlying ostinato of resentment, they have an off-the-cuff feel about them – but that is true of so much of Voltaire. They end in a series of addenda, written in Voltaire's Swiss retreat at *Les Délices*, bringing the story up to date while also suggesting an implicit 'to be continued'. Are they really more about Frederick than Voltaire? Some (like Carlyle) have indeed treated them as a disguised mini-biography of the Prussian King, a view partly shared by Goethe (he thought that Voltaire's gossip on Frederick's sexual tastes was similar to Suetonius on the Roman emperors). Much of Voltaire's life during the period he discusses is omitted from them: there is (no doubt with good reason) little here on some of the most salient episodes of his time in Berlin (his shady financial wheelings and dealings, or his subsequent distressing legal hounding of the businessman Hirschel, whom he seems to have attempted to swindle). Admittedly, they are no more elliptical and selective than most autobiographies. But they are best seen as the memoirs of a relationship – even their last pages return, obsessively, to the 'perfidy' of the King of Prussia, and wonder with grudging admiration what the old fox, whose French poems (some of them daringly anti-Christian, many of them licked into shape by Voltaire himself) had just been published in Paris, would get up to next. Frederick's alert, querulous, domineering, mocking presence haunts these pages almost as much as does Voltaire himself (to whom the same adjectives apply). We do learn about other people who counted in Voltaire's life, but much more tangentially. Madame du Châtelet, for instance, the love of his life, his intellectual partner and fellow student in the latest and most fashionable English science (Newton), is praised for her brilliance (while gently teased for taking Leibniz and other metaphysical systems too seriously: the 'spinning of spiders' webs', Voltaire called it in a letter to Maupertuis). Voltaire's grief at her early death (we know from other sources that, when he staggered out of the room in which she had just died, he was so distraught that he fell down the stairs and cracked his head) is evoked in terms all the more powerful for being laconic. But Voltaire is silent on the stormy ups and downs of their relationship, just as his long affair with his niece, Mme Denis, is barely mentioned. Indeed, in the *Memoirs*, both these women are forced into positions of relative subservience to Frederick, forced to orbit as satellites round the ambiguous gleam of the sun of Potsdam. Madame du Châtelet's role here is essentially to show jealousy when her lover is taken away from her by the King of Prussia; Mme Denis's role is to give her uncle a pretext for expressing even more rage and resentment at their arrest in Frankfurt, on Frederick's orders. *Cherchez la femme* is not good advice for reading the *Memoirs*: there is a love story here, but it is that between Voltaire and Frederick. And like most love stories, it has its initial flirtations, its out-of-the-Prussian-blue *coup de foudre*, its honeymoon, its moments of tranquil contentment overshadowed by the first lovers' tiffs, its increasing tensions, rows and makings up, its petty jealousies and deepening possessiveness, its decline into distance and distaste, its apparent explosive final falling out, and then, once they are safely separated by several hundred leagues, a tentative rapprochement, a mutual curiosity ('what's the old rascal up to now?' they both think), and overtures for peace ('but surely we can still be friends?'). But nothing would heal the trauma left by the infamous scenes of arrest, bureaucratic bullying and real terror inflicted at Frankfurt by the henchmen of the King of Prussia, showing at last who was the *real* master – though Voltaire's behaviour, issuing satirical skits like so many Parthian shots against his erstwhile employer, as he fled back to the unwelcoming embrace of a France from which he was still officially banished, was wonderfully provocative (French and German historians still argue over who comes out of the affair looking worst). From then on, the relationship between them was conducted by letter alone, or mediated by the vast network of gossip that constituted the international Republic of Letters: they never again met.

And it had all started so well! The Francophile Frederick was, even before his accession, cultivating some of the leading French intellectuals of the day with the eventual aim of adorning and enlightening the court of an increasingly self-confident and powerful Prussia; soon he was flirting by letter with Voltaire, whereupon there ensued an exchange of rococo compliments (Voltaire calling Frederick a new Solomon) followed by their first meeting, in Frederick's tumbledown residence in Cleves, on 11th September 1740. As with most accounts of love at first sight, Voltaire's report of this is apparently unreliable (he was, after all, writing nearly twenty years after the event), but oddly poignant: Frederick, in his late twenties, laid low by quartan fever, sweating and shivering in bed, dressed in a shabby blue dressing gown; Voltaire, nearly a score of years older, going over to him and, as it were instinctively, taking the pulse of the man who would never be far out of his thoughts for the next thirty-eight years.

By the time Voltaire had settled down in Berlin, ten years later (he had arrived there on 27th July 1750), had Cupid's darts struck? The two certainly talked the talk. Some allowances must be made for the demonstrative amorousness of male friendship in the age of sensibility. But Frederick was homosexual, and Voltaire (who almost certainly had enjoyed sex with men in earlier years) reminds us of this constantly in the *Memoirs*, in tones that range from the indulgent and complicit (at least one historian thinks he and the King had a real affair) to (much more often) the sly and sardonic. During the first flush of his romance, he was more fulsome: he wrote to his niece that he had been 'formally given away' in marriage to the King of Prussia, and that his heart 'pounded nervously at the altar'… But as the *Memoirs* relate, there was just too much in common between them, over and above their sex, for the *grande passion* between *philosophe* and monarch to last. And Voltaire became increasingly jealous of Maupertuis, whose side Frederick took. Their 'divorce' was inevitable.

Oddly touching though it is, the love story between two brilliant, restless, tetchy men is not the only one related in the *Memoirs*. There is also the love story (always fraught) between the mind that dreams up ideas and the power that enacts them. This is how Voltaire wanted to play it: he was the legislative to Frederick's executive; perhaps he could do more than just polish Frederick's French poetry, and even dissuade him from his unfortunate habit of marching off to war. He so wanted to be Plato to Frederick's Dionysius. But for one thing, as kings go, Frederick, despite being Carlyle's 'terrible practical Doer', was in some ways already quite philosophical enough (even Voltaire, with his watercolour deism, could be – or affected to be – shocked by Frederick's indulgence for the materialist atheism of La Mettrie) – and in any case, he increasingly treated not Voltaire but his rival Maupertuis as his 'Plato' (as Voltaire, with some pique, nicknamed his fellow Frenchman). Nonetheless, the relationship between Voltaire and Frederick seems not just to re-enact the tensions implicit in the idea of the 'philosopher-king', but to anticipate, tentatively and uncertainly, a longing for what would later be called, in language neither of them would probably have liked, the reconciliation of theory and praxis. (Frederick can still be seen trotting merrily along Unter den Linden, whistling the *Hohenfriedberger March*; a short distance away, in the chilly marble of the entrance hall of the Humboldt University, Marx's Eleventh Thesis on Feuerbach still gleams in dull gold.)

And there is yet another fraught relationship running through the *Memoirs*: that between French and German culture. Given the francophilia of Frederick, this produces ironic effects of chiasmus and reflection: at times we are in a vast Hall of Mirrors (which, after all, is where modern Germany was officially to come into being in 1871). Voltaire goes from France to a Prussia whose king is intent on copying French culture; what Voltaire finds in Potsdam is, on a smaller but still impressive scale, Versailles. Frederick speculated that the German language might conceivably develop from boorish peasant grunting into something more civilised, but he far preferred French: Voltaire's attitude to German is best expressed by the names he invented for German characters (Baron von Thunder-ten-tronckh) and places (Valdberghoff-trarbk-dikdorff) in *Candide*. Both of them, convinced that the language of philosophy was French, would have been bemused by what might be called the philosophical tyranny of Germany over France during the last couple of centuries: the Left Bank is watered by the Rhine as much as by the Seine, students in the Sorbonne track Being through the dark thickets of Heideggerean etymontology, and the philosophical revolution wrought by one of Frederick's subjects, Immanuel Kant, still sends shockwaves through the seminar rooms of the Montagne Sainte-Geneviève. It's not all a one-way story: Nietzsche (who dedicated *Human, All-Too-Human* to Voltaire) scorned the culture of the Second Reich and wished he had written *Also sprach Zarathustra* in French; Hegel, like Kant (and Marx) took the French Revolution to be a fateful turning point in modernity, one to which philosophical thinking needed urgently to respond; and even the arch-cantor of Germania, Heidegger, acknowledged his debt to Pascal and (to the continuing surprise of his disciples) praised Descartes (so 'superficial', Nietzsche had sniffed) for his profundity. A historically and politically tragic relationship has proved (not for the first time) unusually productive in philosophy. Voltaire, Frederick, actions, ideas, Germany (or the patchwork congeries of countries that eventually coalesced into Germany), France: a fateful constellation.

I suggested that the *Memoirs* end on a 'could be continued' note. What happened next?

As far as Voltaire was concerned, he was entering his glory days, after the dark, unsettled, nomadic period recorded in the *Memoirs*. In February 1760, the last date recorded in this work, he was already in his mid-sixties, but had only just, in 1759, published *Candide* (a great success, condemned simultaneously by the authorities in Paris and Geneva). In this work he is much meaner to Frederick than in the *Memoirs*, even if he does not name him: the disguise is thin, since the 'King of the Bulgarians' is a transparent swipe at Frederick's sexuality, based on the etymology linking *Bulgarian* with *bugger*, and this warmongering king's soldiers wear blue, like the Prussians. He had ceased his collaboration on the *Encyclopédie*, the first published volumes of which were ordered to be burnt: Frederick was to note in a letter to the *Encyclopédiste* d'Alembert in 1766 that he had heard 'they still burn books in France' – not a bad idea in a cold winter, he added tartly, if there is a shortage of wood; but he would prefer them not to burn the writers, especially not 'certain *philosophes* in whom I still continue to take an interest'. But Voltaire contrived to sustain a European correspondence of heroic proportions, produced some of the works by which he is still best known (the *Dictionnaire philosophique*, *L'Ingénu*, the *Traité sur la Tolérance*), and, from his apparent 'retreat' at *Les Délices* and Ferney, became a one-man Amnesty International, excoriating the powers of State and Church as they continued to inflict horrendous punishments on Calas, Sirven, Espinasse, Lally, Montbailli, D'Etalonde, La Barre (tortured and beheaded: he had, after all, neglected to doff his hat as a Catholic procession went by – a crime compounded by his possessing a copy of… Voltaire's *Dictionnaire philosophique*). He turned into the Voltaire of myth, the Voltaire of 'I disagree with what you say, but I will defend to the death your right to say it' – words he never wrote, but could have. He was given a triumphant reception in Paris when he returned there after nearly three decades of exile in 1778: the crowds hailed the defender of Calas, and the audience crowned him with laurel during a rapturously received performance of his now little-read play *Irène* at the *Théâtre français*. He died shortly after, on 28th May 1778. The *Memoirs*, circulating in pirated form from about 1784 (the date of the first English translation) were published in 1789, a memorable year in every way. When, in July 1791, his body was ceremoniously brought back to Paris for re-interment in the Pantheon, it is said that Louis XVI and Marie-Antoinette watched the procession from behind the shutters of the Tuileries: they were in disgrace with their people, having just tried to escape from their own country.

And Frederick? After the shock of the occupation of Berlin by the Austrians and the Russians in 1760, he managed to keep Prussia going during the Seven Years War, which ended in 1763. He continued to modernise his country. He had already, in 1755, abolished torture, a very Voltairean measure (Voltaire fully expected torture to be definitively abolished during his own lifetime). After their big bust-up, Frederick and Voltaire eyed each other with wary interest as they pursued their epistolary relationship across Europe: indeed, perhaps it was while they were apart that they, independently and yet in an oddly collaborative way, did the most good, with Voltaire writing to question Frederick on his reforms of the legal system and his attitudes to capital punishment, and Frederick assuring Voltaire that his sentencing policy was mildness itself, that it was better for a guilty man to go free than an innocent one be executed... In personal terms, Frederick grew increasingly solitary and inclined to misanthropy, but he still enjoyed boasting to his erstwhile court *philosophe*, in 1777, that agriculture in his domains had made considerable progress, industry was prospering, linen was being exported in large quantities, cobalt was being mined, indigo was being produced, and iron was being turned into steel using a method rather more efficient than the one proposed by the French scientist Réamur. When he heard of Voltaire's death, the King took time off from his latest military campaign to compose an *Eloge de Voltaire*: he also, perhaps as a joke, had Mass said for his dead friend's soul. He himself died in his armchair, on 17th August 1786: his last years had been preoccupied by draining swamps, turning the sterile sands of Brandenburg into land that could feed 7,000 cows, reforming the legal and educational systems, planning repairs to the breaches caused by floods on the Warthe, Vistula and Oder, importing merino lambs into Prussia and planting carrots and turnips. *Il faut cultiver notre jardin*.

– Andrew Brown, 2007

Note on the text

I have used the text in Voltaire, *Mémoires* (Paris: Seuil, 'L'école des lettres', 1993), ed. by Louis Lecomte. The full title of the text reads: *Memoirs to be Used in the Life of M. de Voltaire, Written by Himself*. Much of my background information, as well as some of the material in the notes, is derived from two excellent biographies: *Voltaire Almighty. A Life in Pursuit of Freedom* by Roger Pearson (London: Bloomsbury, 2005), and *Frederick the Great. A Life in Deed and Letters* by Giles MacDonogh (London: Weidenfeld and Nicolson, 1999).

Memoirs of the Life of Monsieur de Voltaire

I was weary of the idle, noisy life of Paris, with all its fops and coxcombs; tired of the dreadful books published with royal approval, the cabals of writers, the low tricks and highway robberies committed by those wretches who dishonoured literature. In 1733, I came across a young woman who more or less shared my opinions, and who decided to go off and spend several years in the country, to cultivate her mind far from the hubbub of the world; she was Mme la Marquise du Châtelet, who of all the women in France was the one with the greatest disposition for all the sciences.[1]

Her father, the Baron de Breteuil, had made her learn Latin, a language which she had mastered as well as Mme Dacier:[2] she knew off by heart the best passages in Horace, Virgil and Lucretius; all of Cicero's philosophical works were familiar to her. She was attracted most of all to mathematics and metaphysics. Few people have combined such perspicacity and taste with such an appetite for knowledge; but she still enjoyed social life and all the amusements of her age and her sex. Nonetheless, she left all that and went off to bury herself away in a dilapidated château on the borders between the Champagne and Lorraine regions, situated on a completely barren and unattractive plot of land. She refurbished this château and embellished it with some quite agreeable gardens. Here I had a gallery built, and turned it into a very fine laboratory for the physical sciences. We installed a well-stocked library there. Several men of learning came to philosophise in our retreat. For two whole years we had the celebrated König,[3] who was a professor at The Hague when he died, and the librarian of the Princess of Orange. Maupertuis[4] came with Jean Bernoulli;[5] from then on, Maupertuis, who had been born the most jealous of men, took me as the object of this passion, which was always so dear to his heart.

I taught Mme du Châtelet English, and after three months she understood it as well as I myself; she could read Locke, Newton and Pope in the original. She learned Italian just as quickly; together, we read all of Tasso and all of Ariosto. So when Algarotti came to Cirey, where he completed his *Neutonianismo per le dame*, he found that she was so competent in his language that she was able to give him some very good advice, from which he profited. Algarotti was a very likeable Venetian, the son of a very wealthy merchant; he travelled all round Europe, knew something about everything, and imbued everything he touched with grace.[6]

In our delightful retreat, we thought only of learning new things, and ignored what was happening in the rest of the world. For a long time, we concentrated mainly on Leibniz and Newton. Madame du Châtelet began by delving into Leibniz, and extended part of his system into a very well-written book called *Institutions de physique*.[7] She did not seek to adorn this philosophy with any embellishments foreign to it; such affectation did not enter into her character, which was masculine and straightforward. Clarity, precision and elegance were the essence of her style. If anyone has been able to lend a certain plausibility to the ideas of Leibniz, it is Mme du Châtelet in this book. But these days, people are starting to lose all interest in what Leibniz might have thought.

She was born for truth, and so she soon abandoned systems of thought and focused on the discoveries of the great Newton. She translated the whole of the *Principia mathematica* into French; and later, when she had broadened and deepened her understanding, she added to this book (which so few people understand) an algebraic commentary which is also above the heads of the common run of readers. Monsieur Clairaut, one of our best geometers, revised this commentary thoroughly.[8]

An edition of it was prepared for publication; it does our century no honour to say that it has not been completed.

At Cirey we cultivated all the arts. There I composed *Alzire*, *Mérope*, *L'Enfant prodigue* and *Mahomet*.[9] For her, I worked on an *Essay on General History* from Charlemagne to the present day: I chose the era of Charlemagne because it was the point at which Bossuet had stopped, and I did not dare touch a period of which that great historian had treated.[10] However, she was not pleased with the *Universal History* written by that prelate. She found it eloquent, but no more; she was indignant that practically the whole of Bossuet's work should dwell on such a contemptible nation as the Jews.

After spending six years in this retreat, amid the arts and sciences, we were obliged to go to Brussels, where the Du Châtelet family had long been involved in a lawsuit against the Honsbrouk family. Here, I had the great good fortune to meet a grandson of the illustrious and ill-fated Grand Pensionary, De Witt, who was now the first president of the Audit Office.[11] He possessed one of the finest libraries in Europe, which was very useful for my *General History*; but in Brussels I had an even rarer stroke of luck that meant more to me: I successfully brought to a conclusion the lawsuit over which the two families had been ruining themselves in costs for sixty years. I saw to it that M. le Marquis du Châtelet was given two hundred and twenty thousand pounds in cash, and as a result, the whole business was settled.

While I was still in Brussels, in 1740, the fat King of Prussia, Frederick William, the most quick-tempered of all kings, unquestionably the most thrifty and the one with the most ready cash, died in Berlin.[12] His son, who has built up such a singular reputation for himself, had been keeping up quite a regular correspondence with me for over four years. There have perhaps never been any father and son in the world who resembled each other less than these two monarchs. The father was a real vandal, whose only thought throughout his reign had been amassing wealth, and maintaining, at the least possible expense to himself, the finest troops in Europe. Never were subjects poorer than his, and never was there a richer king. He had bought up, at knock-down prices, a great part of the lands of his nobles, and they had rapidly squandered the small amount of money they had got in return; and half of this money had flowed back into the king's coffers thanks to the tax he imposed on consumption. All the royal lands were given out to tax collectors who were simultaneously exactors and judges. In consequence, when a farmer had not paid the tax collector by the date appointed, the latter put on his judge's robes and sentenced the delinquent to pay double. It should be pointed out that, when this same judge did not pay the king by the last day of the month, he too was taxed double the amount on the first day of the following month.

If a man killed a hare, lopped off the branches of a tree in the neighbourhood of the king's lands, or committed some other misdemeanour, he had to pay a fine. If an unmarried woman had a child, the mother, or the father, or her parents had to give the king money to preserve appearances.

The Baroness von Knyphausen, the richest widow in Berlin (in other words, she had a private income of between seven and eight thousand pounds), was accused of having given birth to a subject of the King in the second year of her widowhood; the King wrote to her in his own hand saying that, to save her honour, she should immediately send thirty thousand pounds to his treasury; she was obliged to borrow this sum, and was ruined.

There was a minister at The Hague whose name was Luiscius: of all the ministers of crowned heads, he was definitely the one who was worst paid; to keep himself warm, this poor man had a few trees cut down in the garden of Hons-Lardik, which at that time belonged to the royal house of Prussia; shortly afterwards, he received dispatches from his master the King informing him that a year's salary would be docked. Luiscius, thrown into despair, cut his throat with the only razor in his possession: an old valet came to his aid, and unfortunately saved his life. Since then, I have met His Excellency in The Hague, and given him alms at the door of the palace known as the *Old Court*, a palace which belongs to the King of Prussia, and in which this poor ambassador had resided for twelve years.

One has to admit that Turkey is a republic when compared with the despotism exercised by Frederick William. It was by these means that he managed, over a reign of twenty-eight years, to accumulate, in the cellars of his palace in Berlin, around twenty million *écus*, all safely stashed away in barrels with iron hoops. He gave himself the pleasure of furnishing the entire grand apartment of the palace with showy pieces of solid silver, in which art did not manage to impose any form on matter. He also gave his wife the Queen, in account, a cabinet, all the furniture of which was of gold, including the knobs on the end of the coal shovels and fire tongs, and including even the coffee pots.

The monarch would emerge from this palace on foot, dressed in a shabby suit of blue cloth, with brass buttons, that reached halfway down his thighs; and whenever he bought a new suit, he re-used his old buttons. It was in this outfit that His Majesty, armed with a big sergeant's swagger stick, reviewed his regiment of giants every day. This regiment was

his favourite hobby and the pretext for his greatest expenditure. The first rank of his company was composed of men of
whom the shortest was seven foot high: he had these men
bought in the furthest-flung parts of Europe and Asia.[13] I was
still able to see some of them after his death. The King his son,
who liked handsome men, not tall men, had placed them in
the residence of his wife the Queen, to serve as heyducks.[14]
I remember them accompanying an old parade coach that
was sent to pick up the Marquis de Beauvau, who came to
compliment the new king in the November of 1740. The late
King Frederick William, who had previously sold off all of
his father's magnificent furniture, had not been able to let
go of this huge coach, whose gilding had all come off. The
heyducks, who stood by the doors to hold it up in case it fell
over, held hands over the top.

When Frederick William had completed his review, he
went off for a stroll round town; everyone fled as fast as they
could: if he encountered a woman, he would ask her why she
was wasting her time out in the streets. 'Go straight home, you
whore; an honest woman ought to be with her family.' And he
would accompany this rebuke with a hearty slap on the face,
or a kick in the stomach, or a few blows with his stick. This
was also the way he treated the ministers of the Holy Gospel
whenever they felt a desire to go and watch the parade.

One can imagine how amazed and annoyed this vandal
was to have a son who was intelligent, graceful, polite and
eager to please, anxious to learn and a practitioner of music
and poetry. If the King saw a book in the hands of the hereditary Prince, he would fling it into the fire; if the Prince played
the flute, his father would break it, and sometimes insult
His Royal Highness just as he did the ladies and preachers at
the parade.

One fine morning in 1730, the Prince, wearied by all the attention that his father was devoting to him, decided to run away, though he did not yet know whether he would go to England or to France. His father's meanness did not make it possible for him to travel in the style of a farmer general or an English merchant. He borrowed several hundred ducats.

Two very pleasant young men, Katte and Keith, were to accompany him.[15] Katte was the only son of a fine general officer. Keith was the son-in-law of that same Baroness von Knyphausen who had been charged ten thousand *écus* to have children. The date and the hour had been fixed; the father was informed of the whole plan: the Prince and his two travelling companions were arrested simultaneously. At first, the King thought that Princess Wilhelmina, his daughter, who has since married the Prince Margrave of Bayreuth, was in on the plot; and he summarily dispatched the case by kicking her out of a window that was open down to the floor. The Queen Mother, who happened to be present at this dispatch when Wilhelmina was about to fall, just managed to grab her by her skirts. The Princess was left with a contusion underneath her left breast, which she has kept all her life as a mark of her father's feelings for her, and which she did me the honour of showing to me.

The Prince had a kind of mistress, the daughter of a schoolmaster from the town of Brandenburg, whom he had set up at Potsdam. She played the harpsichord, rather badly; the Prince Royal accompanied her on the flute. He thought he was in love with her, but he was mistaken; he had no vocation for her sex. However, as he had pretended to love her, his father made this young lady go round the square in Potsdam, led by the hangman, who gave her a whipping under his son's eyes.[16]

9

After regaling him with this spectacle, his father had Frederick transferred to the citadel of Küstrin, situated in the middle of a marsh. Here he was locked up for six months, without servants, in a kind of prison cell; and after six months he was given a soldier to serve him. This soldier was young, handsome, shapely, and played the flute; he served to pass the prisoner's time in more than one way. All these fine qualities have since made his fortune. I have seen him acting as both a *valet de chambre* and as a prime minister, with all the insolence that these two positions can inspire.

The Prince had been in the castle of Küstrin for a few weeks, when an old officer, followed by four grenadiers, came into his room and burst into tears. Frederick had no doubt but that they had come to cut his throat. But the officer, still weeping, had him taken by the four grenadiers who led him to the window and held his head up while the head of his friend Katte was cut off on a scaffold erected immediately under the window. He held out his hand towards Katte and fainted. His father was present at this spectacle as he had been at that of the whipped girl.

As for Keith, the other confidant, he fled to Holland. The King sent soldiers after him: he got away with just a minute to spare, and embarked for Portugal, where he remained until the death of the merciful Frederick William.

The King had no intention of leaving matters there. He planned to have his son's head cut off. He reflected that he had three other sons, none of whom wrote poetry, and this was quite enough for the glory of Prussia. Measures had already been taken to have the Prince Royal sentenced to death, as had happened to the tsarevich, the elder son of Tsar Peter I.[17]

It does not seem to have been definitively established by human and divine law that a young man should have his head cut off for having shown a desire to travel. But in Berlin, the King would have found judges as skilled at their job as those of Russia. In any case, his paternal authority would have sufficed. Emperor Charles VI, who claimed that the Prince Royal, as a prince of the Empire, could be sentenced to death only at an Imperial Diet, sent the Count of Seckendorff to make the most serious remonstrances to the father. The Count of Seckendorff, whom I have met since in Saxony, where he has retired, swore to me that he had had the greatest difficulty in ensuring that the Prince's head would not be cut off. It was this same Seckendorff who commanded the armies of Bavaria; the Prince, when he became King of Prussia, portrays him in a dreadful light in the history of his father, which he inserted into some thirty copies of his *Memoirs of Brandenburg*.* And the moral of this is: serve princes, and ensure that nobody cuts off their heads.

After eighteen months, the appeals of the Emperor and the tears of the Queen of Prussia won the hereditary Prince his freedom. He started to compose poetry and music more than ever. He read Leibniz, and even Wolff, whom he called a compiler of nonsense,[18] and he dabbled in all the sciences at once, to the best of his ability.

As his father did not allow him to take part much in business, and as there was not much business to be done in this country, where everything consisted of military parades, he spent his leisure time writing to all the men of letters in France who enjoyed any degree of reputation. The main burden fell upon me. There were verse letters; there were treatises on metaphysics, history and politics. He called me a divine man; I called him a Solomon. These epithets cost us nothing. Some

* I gave the Elector Palatine the copy which the King of Prussia presented to me. (*Voltaire's note*.)

of this twaddle was published in my collected works; fortunately, what was published was less than a thirtieth part of the total. I took the liberty of sending him a very fine escritoire by Martin; he was so kind as to send me a few trinkets in amber. And the wits in the cafés of Paris were horror-stricken at the thought that my fortune was made.

A young man from Courland, Keyserlingk by name, who also wrote moderately good French poetry, and was in consequence his favourite at the time, was sent from the borders of Pomerania to Cirey, where we feted his arrival: I put on a display of fireworks for him, which spelled out the name and initials of the Prince Royal, with this motto: *The hope of the human race*. For my part, if I had been so bold as to conceive of any personal hopes, I was more than entitled to do so: the letters sent to me began *My dear friend*, and I was often told, in these missives, of the solid proofs of friendship that would indubitably follow once my correspondent was enthroned. And enthroned he finally was while I was in Brussels; the first thing he did was to send to France, as an ambassador extraordinary, a one-armed man named Camas, who had previously been a French refugee, and was now an officer in his troops. He said that there was a French minister in Berlin who had only one hand, and that, to acquit himself of all that he owed the King of France, he was sending him an ambassador who had only one arm. When Camas arrived at the inn, he sent a young man to me, whom he had made his page, to say that he was too tired to come to my house; he requested that I visit him in his lodgings on the hour, and he had the biggest and most magnificent present to give me on behalf of the King his master. 'Run along,' said Mme du Châtelet; 'they must have sent you the crown jewels.' I ran along and found the ambassador, whose only luggage, standing behind his chair, was

12

a quarter cask of wine from the cellar of the late King, which the present King ordered me to drink. I soon ran out of expressions of amazement and gratitude at the liquid marks of His Majesty's favours, a substitute for the solid marks with which he had flattered my hopes, and I shared the quarter cask with Camas.

My Solomon was at that time in Strasbourg. He had dreamt up the idea, as he visited his long, narrow States, from Guelders to the Baltic Sea, of seeing the frontiers and troops of France incognito.

He gave himself this pleasure in Strasbourg, under the assumed name of the Comte du Four, a rich lord of Bohemia. His brother, the Prince Royal, who was accompanying him, had also assumed a *nom de guerre*; and Algarotti, who had attached himself to Frederick, was the only one not travelling in disguise.

The King sent to me in Brussels an account of his trip, half in prose and half in verse, in a style that approximated that of Bachaumont and Chapelle,[19] at least, as much as a King of Prussia can approximate such poets. Here are a few passages from his letter:

After some dreadful roads, we found lodgings that were even more dreadful.

   For our selfish hosts,
   Seeing us famished as ghosts,
   In a fashion more than frugal,
   In a hovel quite infernal,
   Stole all our money as they poisoned us.
   How different from the age of Lucullus! [20]

Terrible roads; awful food, awful drink; that was not the least
of it: we met with several accidents; and indeed, our retinue
must have looked distinctly odd, since in every place through
which we passed, we were taken to be something quite different.

Some thought we must be royalty;
Some thought we were quite rascally;
And some thought we were men of learning.
Sometimes the people all came running
And stared at us quite haughtily,
Filled with impertinent curiosity.

The master of the post stage at Kehl assured us there was
no salvation without a passport, and seeing that we were
thus placed in the absolute necessity of making passports
for ourselves, or never entering Strasbourg, we were
obliged to take the first option, in which the Prussian coat
of arms on my seal was of enormous help.

We arrived in Strasbourg, and the corsair at the
customs house and the inspector seemed happy with
the proof of our identity.

And so those scoundrels looked us up and down;
With one eye read our passports with a frown
While with the other they weighed up our purse.
In times like this, gold is the best resource;
When Jupiter did wish to make so bold
With Danaë, he showered her with gold;
Gold made great Caesar of the whole world lord;
Gold, more than Mars or Venus, is adored;
And gold it was that gave us hospitality
That night within the walls of Strasbourg city.

As this letter shows, Frederick had not yet become quite the best of our poets, and his philosophy was not altogether immune to the metal that his father had amassed.

From Strasbourg he went to see his States in Lower Germany, and sent me a message saying that he would come to see me incognito in Brussels. We prepared a fine house for him to stay in; but he fell ill in the little château of Meuse, two leagues from Cleves, and wrote to tell me that he expected me to take the initiative. So I went to pay him my profoundest homage. Maupertuis, who already had his own opinions, and was completely obsessed by the idea of being president of some academy, had already gone to introduce himself, and was lodging with Algarotti and Keyserlingk in an attic room in this palace. The only guard I found at the gate was a single soldier. The privy councillor Rambonet, Minister of State, was walking up and down in the courtyard, blowing on his fingers. He was wearing big, scruffy, canvas sleeves, a hat with holes in it, and an old magistrate's wig, one end of which fell into one of his pockets, while the other hardly came down past his shoulder. I was told that this man was entrusted with an important piece of State business; and this was true.

I was led into His Majesty's apartment. There was nothing there but the four walls. In a recess, I suddenly saw, by the light of a candle, a narrow pallet two and a half feet wide, on which lay a short man in a dressing gown of coarse blue cloth: this was the King, sweating and shivering under a shabby blanket, suffering from a violent fit of fever. I bowed to him, and struck up an acquaintance with him by taking his pulse, as if I had been his first doctor. Once the fever fit had passed, he dressed and sat down at table. Algarotti, Keyserlingk, Maupertuis and the King's Minister to the States General were with us at supper, and discussed in depth the topics of the immortality of the soul, freedom, and the androgynous creatures in Plato.

All this time, Councillor Rambonet was riding on a hired horse: he travelled all night, and the next day he arrived at the gates of Liège, where he gave orders in the name of His Majesty the King, while two thousand men from the troops of Wesel ransacked the city of Liège. The alleged object of this extraordinary urgency was some rights that the King claimed over a certain part of town. He even entrusted me with composing a manifesto, and I duly wrote a tolerably good one, never doubting but that a king with whom I dined and who called me his friend must always be right. The business was soon settled, thanks to a million ducats in weight that he requested, and which served to indemnify him for the costs of his journey to Strasbourg, of which he had complained so poetically in his letter.

I could not help but feel drawn to him, since he was intelligent and graceful and was, furthermore, a king, which is always something very seductive, given human weakness. Usually it is we writers who flatter kings; here was a king praising me from my head to my feet, while the Abbé Desfontaines and other rascals were slandering me in Paris at least once a week.[21]

Some time before his father's death, the King of Prussia had taken it into his head to write against the principles of Machiavelli. If Machiavelli had had a prince as his disciple, the first thing he would have recommended would have been that the prince write against him. But the Prince Royal had not imagined such subtleties. He had written in good faith, when he was not yet a sovereign, and when his father inspired him with no love for the powers of a despot. So he praised moderation and justice with all his heart, and in his enthusiasm,

he regarded all usurpation as a crime. He had sent his manuscript to me in Brussels, to correct it and get it published; and
I had already presented it to a bookseller in Holland named
Van Duren, the most illustrious rascal of his kind. I was later
filled with compunction at having aided the publication of
the *Anti-Machiavelli*, while the King of Prussia, who had a
hundred million in his coffers, was taking one million from the
poor Liégeois by the hand of councillor Rambonet. I judged
that my Solomon would not leave it at that. His father had left
him excellent troops – sixty-six thousand, four hundred men
in total; he was increasing their number, and seemed to be
quite willing to use them at the earliest opportunity.

I pointed out to him that it was not perhaps the right thing
to have his book published at exactly the same time he could
be accused of violating its precepts. He allowed me to stop
it being printed. I went to Holland with the sole purpose of
doing him this small favour; but the bookseller requested so
much money that the King, who in any case was, in his heart
of hearts, not at all displeased to see himself in print, preferred
to be published for free than to have to pay not to be published.

While I was in Holland busy with this task, Emperor
Charles VI died, in October 1740, of indigestion caused by
mushrooms which led to an apoplectic fit; and that plate of
mushrooms changed the destiny of Europe.[22] It soon became
apparent that Frederick II, King of Prussia, was not such an
enemy of Machiavelli as the Prince Royal had been. Although
he was already hatching his plan to invade Silesia, he
nonetheless summoned me to his court.

I had already intimated to him that I could not settle there
forever, that I was bound to prefer friendship to ambition, that
I was attached to Mme du Châtelet, and that, philosopher for
philosopher, I preferred a lady to a king.

He approved of this liberty, even though he did not like women. I went to pay court to him in October.

The Cardinal de Fleury[23] wrote me a long letter filled with praise for the *Anti-Machiavelli* and its author; I did not fail to show this letter to Frederick. He was already assembling his troops, though none of his generals nor his ministers was able to fathom his plans. The Marquis de Beauvau, sent as an envoy to compliment him on his accession, thought he would declare against France in favour of Maria Theresa, Queen of Hungary and Bohemia, daughter of Charles VI; that he wished to support the election to the Imperial throne of François de Lorraine, Grand Duke of Tuscany, the husband of this queen; and that he might well find it greatly to his advantage to do so.

I more than anyone should have been inclined to think that the new king of Prussia was indeed going to bend this way, since he had sent me, three months previously, a piece of political writing in his usual style, in which he regarded France as the natural enemy and despoiler of Germany. But it was in his nature always to do the opposite of what he said and wrote – not out of dissimulation, but because he wrote and spoke under the impulse of one kind of enthusiasm, and then acted under another.

He left on 15th December, with a quartan fever, to conquer Silesia, at the head of thirty thousand soldiers, well-provisioned and well-disciplined; as he mounted his horse, he said to the Marquis de Beauvau, 'I'm going to play your game; if I draw the aces, we'll share the winnings.'

He has since written the story of that conquest; he showed the whole thing to me. Here is one of the curious articles from the start of those annals; I took care to transcribe it first, as being a unique memorial.

'To these considerations add that I had troops always ready to act, a well-stocked treasury and a vivacious character: these were the reasons I had for waging war on Maria Theresa, Queen of Bohemia and Hungary.' And a few lines later, there came these very words: 'Ambition, self-interest, and the desire to make people talk about me, won the day; and I resolved to go to war.'

Ever since there have been conquerors, or ardent spirits desirous of being conquerors, I think he is the first to have done himself justice in this way. Never, perhaps, has a man sensed more clearly what was reasonable, and yet listened only to his passions. This combination of philosophy and an unbridled imagination has always been the essence of his character.

It is a pity that I got him to cut this passage when I later corrected all of his works: such a rare confession should have been transmitted to posterity, as a demonstration of the basis on which almost all wars are fought. We writers, poets, historians, declaimers in the academies, celebrate those grand exploits: and here we have a king carrying them out, and yet condemning them.

His troops were already in Silesia when Baron Gotter, his minister in Vienna, quite uncivilly proposed to Maria Theresa that she in all good grace surrender to the King Elector, her master,[24] three quarters of that province; if she agreed, the King of Prussia would lend her three million *écus*, and make her husband Emperor.

Maria Theresa had at that time neither troops, nor money, nor credit; and yet she proved inflexible. She preferred to risk losing everything rather than to bow before a prince whom she regarded as a mere vassal of her ancestors, and whose life the Emperor her father had saved. Her generals could barely scrape together twenty thousand men; her marshal Neipperg, their commander, forced the King of Prussia to accept battle before the walls of Neisse, at Mollwitz.[25] The Prussian cavalry was initially routed by the Austrian cavalry; and at the first shock, the King, who was not yet accustomed to seeing battles, fled all the way to Oppeln, a good twelve leagues away from the battlefield. Maupertuis, who had imagined he would make a great fortune, had followed with the King's retinue on this campaign, thinking that the King would at least ensure he was provided with a horse. This was not the King's custom. Maupertuis bought a donkey for two ducats on the day of the action, and started to follow His Majesty, on his donkey, as best he could. His mount was unable to keep up; he was seized and robbed by the hussars.

Frederick spent the night on a pallet in a village inn near Ratibor, on the borders of Poland. He was in despair, and thought he would now be reduced to crossing Poland to re-enter the northern part of his States; but then one of his footmen arrived from the camp at Mollwitz and announced that he had won the battle. This news was confirmed a quarter of an hour later by an aide-de-camp. The news was correct. While the Prussian cavalry had been weak, the infantry was the best in Europe. It had been disciplined over thirty years by the old Prince von Anhalt. The Marshall von Schwerin, its commander, was a pupil of Charles XII; he won the battle as soon as the King of Prussia had fled the field. The monarch returned the next day, and the victorious general was more or less dismissed from court.

I returned to philosophise in my retreat at Cirey. I spent the winters in Paris, where I had a host of enemies: as, a long time previously, I had decided to write the *History of Charles XII*, as well as putting on various plays and even composing an epic poem, I found – as one might expect – that all those who took an interest in poetry and prose became my persecutors. And as I had even been so bold as to write on philosophy, it was inevitable that those people who go by the name of *dévots* would call me an atheist, as long-standing custom dictated.[26]

I had been the first who had dared to reveal Newton's discoveries to my nation in intelligible language. The Cartesian prejudices that had in France succeeded the prejudices of the Aristotelian school were at that time so deeply rooted that Chancellor d'Aguesseau regarded as an enemy of reason and State anyone who adopted any of the discoveries that had been made in England. He was never willing to grant permission for my *Elements of Newton's Philosophy* to be published.[27]

I was a great admirer of Locke: I regarded him as the only sensible metaphysician; I especially praised the restraint – so new, so wise and at the same time so bold – with which he says that we will never know enough by the light of mere reason to assert that God cannot grant the gift of feeling and thought to the being known as *matter*.

It is difficult to imagine the bitterness and the inexorable ignorance that was unleashed on me as a result of this article. Locke's 'feeling' had not hitherto made much of a stir in France, since the learned folk read Saint Thomas and Quesnel,[28] and the ordinary run of people read novels. Once I had praised Locke, there was an outcry against him and against me. The poor folk who got carried away in this quarrel cannot have known what *matter* is, nor what is *mind*. The fact is that we know nothing of ourselves, that we have movement, life, feeling and thought without knowing how; the elements of matter are just as unknown to us as all the rest; we are blind men, feeling our way along and reasoning in the

21

dark; and Locke was extremely wise in admitting that it is not for us to decide what the Almighty cannot do.

This, together with the success of a few of my plays, brought down on my head a whole huge library of pamphlets in which it was proved that I was a bad poet, an atheist and the son of a peasant.

My life story was published, including this fine genealogy. A German did not fail to gather together all the tales of this kind with which the lampoons published against me were stuffed. I was accused of getting involved with people whom I had never met, and with others who had never existed.

As I write this, I have before me a letter from M. le Maréchal de Richelieu, informing me of a gross lampoon in which it was proved that his wife had given me a fine coach, and something else besides, at a time when he had no wife. I had initially taken pleasure in making a collection of these calumnies; but they became so numerous that I gave up.

That was the only fruit I had harvested from my labours. I was easily consoled, sometimes in my retreat at Cirey and sometimes in the good company I could find in Paris.

While the shitbags of literature were thus waging war on me, France was waging war on the Queen of Hungary, and one has to admit that this war had no more justice behind it: for, after having solemnly stipulated, guaranteed and sworn to the Pragmatic Sanction of Emperor Charles VI,[29] and the succession of Maria Theresa to her father's throne, and after having received Lorraine in return for these promises, it did not seem entirely in conformity with people's rights to break such a commitment. The Cardinal de Fleury was caught up in the affray. He could not claim, like the King of Prussia, that it was the vivacity of his temperament that had led him to take up arms. This happy priest was still ruling at the age of eighty-six years, and holding the reins of State in his very feeble hands. Forces had been joined with the King of Prussia while he was conquering Silesia; two armies had been sent to Germany at a time when Maria Theresa had none. One of these armies had penetrated to within five leagues of Vienna without encountering any enemies: Bohemia had been given to the Elector of Bavaria, who was elected Emperor after having been appointed Lieutenant General of the armies of the King of France. But soon, people were making exactly the mistakes that were bound to lead to the loss of everything.

The King of Prussia's courage had in the meantime ripened, and he had won some battles; now he made peace with the Austrians. Maria ceded, to her very great regret, the county of Glatz with Silesia. Having detached himself from France on these conditions without further ado, in June 1742, he wrote to tell me that he was now convalescing, and advised the other patients to get well soon.

This prince was now at the height of his powers, with one hundred and thirty thousand victorious soldiers at his command, from which he had built up the cavalry, and drawing from Silesia twice as much as that region had produced for the house of Austria; he was firmly established in his new conquests, and all the happier because every other power was suffering. These days, princes are ruined by war; he had grown rich on it.

His attention now turned to embellishing the city of Berlin, building one of the finest opera houses in Europe and summoning artists of every kind, for he wished to take every road to glory and obtain it as cheaply as possible.

His father had lodged at Potsdam in a shabby house; he turned it into a palace. Potsdam became an attractive town. Berlin was growing; people were starting to enjoy some of the comforts and pleasures of life that the late king had sorely neglected: some people had furniture; most of them even wore shirts – for during the previous reign, people barely had more than shirt fronts that were tied together with strings; and the reigning King had not been brought up any differently. Things were changing as you watched: Sparta became Athens. Deserts were reclaimed and one hundred and three villages were built in drained swamps. He still continued to make music and write books: so he had no reason for being annoyed with me for calling him the Solomon of the North. I gave him this sobriquet in my letters, and it stuck with him for a long time.

Affairs in France were at that time not as good as his. He enjoyed the secret pleasure of seeing the French perishing in Germany, after their military diversion had enabled him to conquer Silesia. The court of France was losing its troops, its money, its glory and its credit, since it had made Charles VII emperor; and this emperor was losing everything, since he had believed that the French would support him.

The Cardinal de Fleury died on 29th January 1743, at the age of ninety years: never had anyone been appointed a minister any later in life, and never had a minister kept his position for longer. His fortunes began at the age of seventy-three when he became King of France, and he remained so until his death, without contradiction, always affecting the greatest modesty, amassing no wealth, refraining from any display and limiting himself to the sole task of reigning. He left behind him the reputation of being a discerning and likeable man rather than a genius, and was considered to have been better acquainted with the Court than with Europe.

I had the honour of seeing him a great deal at the home of Mme la Maréchale de Villars, when he was merely an ex-bishop of the unattractive little town of Fréjus, of which he had always labelled himself *bishop by divine indignation*, as can be seen in several of his letters. Fréjus was a very ugly woman whom he had spurned at the earliest possible opportunity. The Maréchal de Villeroi, who did not know that the Bishop had long been the lover of his wife the Maréchale, had him appointed by Louis XIV as private tutor to Louis XV; from tutor he rose to prime minister, and did not fail to contribute to the exiling of the Maréchal his benefactor. Apart from being ungrateful, he was quite a decent man. But as he was not himself talented, he kept all those who were talented, in any shape or form, at arm's length.

Several Academicians put it about that I was after his place in the French Academy. At the King's supper, the question was asked as to who would deliver the funeral oration of the Cardinal de Fleury at the Academy. The King replied that it would be myself. His mistress, the Duchesse de Châteauroux, was in favour; but the Comte de Maurepas, Secretary of State, was not. He had the obstinate habit of quarrelling with all his master's mistresses, and this was a mistake.

An old fool named Boyer, the Dauphin's tutor, who had previously been a Theatine[30] and later Bishop of Mirepoix, took it on himself to follow the dictates of his conscience and to support the whim of M. de Maurepas. This Boyer was in charge of the portfolio of benefices; the King left him to deal with all the affairs of the clergy: he treated this one as a point of ecclesiastical discipline. He made out that it would be an offence to God if a profane person like myself were to succeed a cardinal. I knew that M. de Maurepas was egging him on; I went to see this minister; I told him: 'A place in the Academy is not a particularly important dignity; but once one has been nominated for it, it is depressing not to get it. You have quarrelled with Madame de Châteauroux, whom the King loves, and with Monsieur le Duc de Richelieu, whom she obeys; what, may I ask, do your quarrels have to do with an insignificant seat in the French Academy? I beg you to give me a frank answer: if Madame de Châteauroux wins out over the Bishop of Mirepoix, will you oppose her...?' He thought it over for a few moments and then told me: '*Yes, and I will crush you.*'

The priest finally won out over the mistress; and I did not get the place in the Academy that I did not particularly want. I like to recall this episode, as it demonstrates how petty those we call 'great' can be, and indicates how important unimportant trifles can sometimes seem to them.

Meanwhile, affairs of State had not been going any better since the death of the Cardinal than during his last two years. The house of Austria was rising anew from its ashes. France was under pressure from both Austria and England. So there remained nothing else for us but to fall back on the King of Prussia, who had dragged us into war and then abandoned us when things got difficult.

A plan was hatched to send me secretly to this monarch to sound out his intentions, and see whether he would be in a mood to forestall the storms that were bound to fall from Vienna upon him, sooner or later, after falling upon us, and whether he might not be willing to lend us one hundred thousand men, at this juncture, to secure Silesia for him. This idea had come into the heads of M. Richelieu and Mme de Châteauroux. The King adopted it; and M. Amelot, Minister of Foreign Affairs, albeit a very junior minister, was simply entrusted with the task of expediting my departure.

A pretext was needed. The one I chose was that of my quarrel with the ex-Bishop of Mirepoix. The King gave his approval to this stratagem. I wrote to the King of Prussia saying that I could no longer put up with the persecutions of this Theatine, and that I intended to take refuge with a philosopher king, far from that bothersome bigot. As this prelate still signed his name in abbreviated form: *anc. évêque de Mirepoix*, and his handwriting was rather scrawling, it could be read: *L'âne de Mirepoix* instead of *l'ancien*:[31] this caused considerable merriment; never were negotiations more light-hearted.

The King of Prussia, who launched himself into an all-out attack whenever it was a matter of striking at monks and prelates at Court, wrote back with a whole flood of mocking banter on *l'âne de Mirepoix*, and urged me to come. I took considerable pains to ensure that my letters and his replies were read by others. The Bishop was informed. He went to Louis XV to complain that I was, as he said, making him appear foolish in foreign courts. The King replied that agreement had already been reached on the matter, and he should take no notice.

Louis XV's reply was really not in character and has always struck me as quite extraordinary. At one and the same time I had the pleasure of avenging myself on the Bishop who had excluded me from the Academy, that of taking a very pleasant trip abroad and that of being in a position to perform a service for my King and country. Monsieur de Maurepas himself took a warm interest in the proceedings, since at that time he told M. Amelot what to do, and thought that he himself was really the Minister for Foreign Affairs.

The strangest thing is that it was necessary to let Mme de Châtelet in on the secret. She was quite unwilling, for whatever price, for me to leave her for the King of Prussia; she thought there was nothing so cowardly and hateful in all the world as for a man to leave a woman for a monarch. She would have made the most terrible fuss. In order to keep her quiet, we decided to let her in on the mystery, and agreed that the letters would pass through her hands.

I was given all the money I wanted for my trip, in return for a simple receipt, from M. de Montmartel. I did not squander it. I stayed for a short time in Holland, while the King of Prussia hurried from one end of his States to the other, getting up revenue. My stay in The Hague was equally useful. I lodged in the palace of the Old Court, which at that time belonged to the King of Prussia through his sharing arrangements with the House of Orange. His envoy, the young Count von Podewils, who loved and was loved by the wife of one of the principal members of State, managed, by the good offices of the lady in question, to pick up copies of all the secret resolutions of Their Most Puissant Personages, filled with malicious intent towards us. I sent these copies to the French Court; and this was a most agreeable service for me to perform.

When I arrived in Berlin, the King lodged me in his palace, as he had done on my previous trips. In Potsdam he led the same life that he always led after his accession to the throne. It is worth going into the small details of this:

He would get up at five o'clock in the morning in summer, and at six in winter. If you would like to know the royal ceremonies that graced this *lever*, what the great and the little *entrées* consisted in, the functions of his grand chaplain, his grand chamberlain, his first gentleman of the chamber and his ushers, I can tell you that a lackey came to light his fire, dress him and shave him; even so, he dressed himself pretty much alone. His bedroom was quite handsome; a rich balustrade of silver, decorated with little cherubs, very finely sculpted, seemed to enfold the dais of a bed whose curtains were visible;

but behind the curtains there was, at the foot of the bed, a set of bookshelves; and as for the King's bed, it was a low camp bed with a thin mattress, hidden by a screen. Marcus Aurelius and Julian, his two apostles and the greatest men of Stoicism, had beds no more modest than his.

When His Majesty was dressed and his boots were on, the Stoic would give a few minutes to the sect of Epicurus: he had two or three of his favourites come in – either lieutenants of his regiment, or pageboys, or heyducks or young cadets. They drank coffee. The one to whom a handkerchief was thrown stayed for a few minutes in private with the King. Things could never go all the way, given that, while his father had still been alive, the Prince had suffered greatly as a result of his passing fancies, and had never really been cured. He could not play the principal role; he had to be content with a secondary part.

Once these schoolboy frolics were over, affairs of State took their place. His Prime Minister entered via a hidden flight of stairs, with a big bundle of papers under his arm. This Prime Minister was a clerk who lived on the second floor in the house of Fredersdorf, the soldier who had become a *valet de chambre* and a favourite, and had previously served the King when he was a prisoner in the castle at Küstrin. The secretaries of State sent all their reports in to the King's clerk. He brought a summary of them with him: the King had the answers written in the margin, in just a couple of words. In this way all the affairs of the kingdom were expedited in an hour. The secretaries of State and the ministers in charge rarely saw him in person: indeed, there were some to whom he had never spoken. The King his father had put financial matters in such good order, everything was carried out with such military precision, and obedience was so blind, that four hundred leagues' worth of country were governed like an abbey.

At around eleven o'clock, the King, in his boots, reviewed his regiment of guards in his garden; and, at the same hour, all the colonels did exactly the same in every province. In the interval between the parade and dinner, the princes his brothers, the generals and one or two chamberlains ate at his table; the food was as good as it can be in a country where there is neither game, nor any passable meat, nor any fattened pullets, and where the wheat has to be brought in from Magdeburg.

After the meal, he withdrew to the solitude of his private apartment, where he wrote poetry until five or six o'clock. Then a young man called Darget arrived; he had previously been the secretary of Valori, the French envoy; he now read to Frederick. A little concert began at seven o'clock: the King played the flute as well as the best musician. The performers often played his compositions; there was no art that he did not cultivate, and among the Greeks he would not have been forced to make the humiliating confession of Epaminondas, that he did not know music.[32]

Supper was served in a small room whose most singular adornment was a painting which he had asked Pesne, his painter, one of our best colourists, to design. It was a fine *priapea*, depicting young men embracing women, nymphs recumbent under satyrs, cupids playing the game of Encolpius and Giton,[33] several persons gazing in fainting languor at these amorous combats, turtle doves kissing, he-goats mounting nanny-goats and rams tupping ewes.

The meals too were often just as philosophical. If anyone had eavesdropped on our conversation, while gazing at this painting, he would have thought he was overhearing the Seven Sages of Greece in the brothel. Nowhere in the world did people ever speak more freely of all the superstitions of men, and never were these treated with more mockery and contempt. God was respected, but all those who had deceived mankind in his name were scorned.

Women and priests were never admitted into the palace. In a word, Frederick lived without court, without councillors and without religion.

Some provincial judges wanted to burn some poor peasant accused by a priest of an amorous dalliance with his she-ass: nobody could be executed unless the King had confirmed the sentence – a most humane law, practised in England and certain other countries; Frederick wrote, at the bottom of the sentence, that in his States he granted *freedom of conscience and p...*[34]

A priest from near Stettin, quite scandalised by this indulgence, slipped into his sermon on Herod a few details that might have been taken to characterise the King his master. Frederick ordered this village parson to Potsdam, summoning him before the consistory, although there was no more of a consistory at court than there was any celebration of Mass. The poor man was brought to Potsdam: the King put on the robes and clerical bands of a preacher; d'Argens, the author of the *Jewish Letters*, and a certain Baron Pöllnitz who had changed religion three or four times, dressed in the same outfit;[35] they placed a volume of Bayle's *Dictionary*[36] on a table, as if it were the Gospels, and the defendant was brought in by two grenadiers to face these three ministers of the Lord. 'My brother,' said the King to him, 'let me ask you in God's name which was the Herod on whom you preached...'

'It was the Herod who had the little children killed,' the man replied.

'Let me ask you,' added the King, 'if it was Herod the first of that name, for as you must know, there were several.'

The village parson had no idea what to reply.

'What!' said the King, 'You dare to preach on a certain Herod, and you do not know to which family he belonged! You are unworthy of your sacred ministry. We will pardon you this once; but know that we will excommunicate you if ever you preach on anyone without knowing his full identity.'

Thereupon they delivered his sentence and pardoned him. They signed with three ridiculous names they had dreamt up for the occasion.

'Tomorrow we shall be going to Berlin,' added the King; 'we will ask for mercy for you from our brothers: do not fail to come and speak to us.' The priest went round Berlin looking for the three ministers: everyone laughed at him; and the King, who enjoyed a joke but was no liberal, did not even bother to pay his travel expenses.

Frederick governed the Church as despotically as he did the State. It was he who sanctioned divorces when a husband and a wife wished to marry other people. One day, a minister quoted to him what the Old Testament has to say on such divorces. 'Moses,' he replied, 'led his Jews just as he wanted, and I will govern my Prussians as I see fit.'

This singular way of governing, this even stranger way of life, this contrasting mixture of Stoicism and Epicureanism, of severity in military discipline and self-indulgence within his palace, the pageboys with whom he amused himself in his private apartment and the soldiers who had to run the gauntlet thirty-six times under the King's windows as he watched them, moralising speeches and unbridled licentiousness, all formed a bizarre picture, which few people at the time knew of, and which has since spread across Europe.

The greatest thrift presided over all of his tastes at Potsdam. His table, and that of his officers and servants, were fixed at thirty-three *écus* per day, wine not included. And whereas, in the case of other kings, it is officers of the Crown who take charge of this expenditure, it was his *valet de chambre* Fredersdorf who was simultaneously his grand major-domo, his grand cup-bearer and his grand pantler.

Either through a sense of thrift or of politics, he did not grant the least favour to his ex-favourites, especially to those who had risked their lives for him when he was Prince Royal. He did not even pay back the money he had borrowed at that time; and just as Louis XII did not avenge the insults to the Duc d'Orléans, the King of Prussia forgot the debts of the Prince Royal.[37]

That poor mistress who had been whipped by the executioner because of him, was at that time living in Berlin, married to the clerk in charge of the bureau of *fiacres* (there were eighteen *fiacres* in Berlin); and her lover gave her a pension of seventy *écus*, which was always paid perfectly regularly. Her name was Mme Shommers; a tall, thin woman, who looked like a sibyl and not at all like a woman who had deserved to be whipped for a prince.

However, whenever he went to Berlin, he would put on a magnificent display on ceremonial days. It was a very fine spectacle for men of vanity (in other words for practically everyone) to see him sitting at table, surrounded by twenty princes of the Empire, served from the finest gold plate in Europe, and thirty handsome pageboys, with an equal number of young heyducks superbly apparelled, carrying great dishes of solid gold. The great officers would also appear, and these were the only occasions on which they were ever seen.

After dinner they would go to the Opera, that great hall three hundred feet long, which one of his chamberlains, Knobelsdorff by name, had built without an architect. The finest voices and the best dancers were in his employ. La Barberina danced on his stage: it was she who later married the son of his chancellor. The King had caused this dancer to be abducted from Venice by soldiers who brought her (via Vienna) to Berlin. He was somewhat in love with her, as she had the legs of a man. What was quite incomprehensible was that he paid her a salary of thirty-two thousand pounds.

His Italian poet, who put into verse the operas for which the King himself always provided the storyline, earned only one thousand two hundred pounds; but one needs to bear in mind that he was terribly ugly, and could not dance. In a word, La Barberina all alone earned more than three Ministers of State put together. As for the Italian poet, he took matters into his own hands and paid himself: he unsewed some of the old gold braid with which a chapel of the First King of Prussia was decorated. The King, who never went to chapel, said he had not lost anything. In any case, he had just written a Dissertation in Favour of Thieves, printed in the collections of his Academy; and for once he did not think it was a good idea to belie his writings by his deeds.

This indulgence did not extend to the military. There was in the prisons of Spandau an old gentleman of Franche-Comté, six feet tall, whom the late King had caused to be abducted for his imposing stature; he had been promised a place as chamberlain, and instead they gave him one as a soldier. This poor man soon deserted with several of his comrades; he was captured and brought back to face the late King, to whom he was naive enough to say that his only regret was that he had not killed a tyrant like him. In response, they cut off his nose and his ears; he ran the gauntlet thirty-six times; after which, he went off to do hard labour in Spandau.

He was still there when M. de Valori, our envoy, urged me to beg the most clement son of the most harsh Frederick William for mercy on his behalf. It pleased His Majesty to say that it was for me that he had *La Clemenza di Tito* performed – an opera full of beautiful passages by the celebrated Metastasio, set to music by the King himself with the help of his composer.[38] I took the trouble to commend to his kindness the poor man from Franche-Comté without ears or nose, and I fired off this reprimand:

Great genius, noble mind and tender heart!
Although you reign, you have not found the art
Of bringing to an end the grief and woe
That never cease to plague your subjects so.

With trembling lips around you stand the Prayers
Who rule great souls. They are remorse's heirs:
Aghast they find that they must shed vain tears
On hands that should have calmed all earth's dark fears.

Is it for me you're putting on this show?
How splendid! – La Clemenza di Tito!
But you should Titus' mercy also mimic:
Without its moral, opera's just a gimmick.

The petition was rather direct; but one has the right to say anything one wants in poetry. The King promised to alleviate the prisoner's plight somewhat; and indeed, several months later, he was so kind as to place the gentleman in question in the hospice, at a cost of six *sous* per day. He had refused this favour to his mother the Queen; apparently she had made her request in mere prose.

Amid the parties, the operas and the suppers, my secret negotiations made progress. The King thought it would be a good idea if I could tell him everything, and I often raised questions about France and Austria when we were discussing the *Aeneid* and Livy. The conversation would sometimes grow animated: the King became heated, and told me that, so long as our court knocked at every door to obtain peace, he would not take it into his head to fight for it. From my room I sent to him in his apartment my reflections on sheets of paper with narrow margins. He would fill these with a column of answers to my daring questions. I still have the paper in which I asked him: 'Do you think that the House of Austria will request you to hand back Silesia at the first opportunity?' Here is the reply he wrote in the margin:

An answer I will send
But fences never mend
My friend.

This quite novel form of negotiation ended with a speech he came out with, when feeling particularly inspired, against the King of England, his dear uncle. These two kings did not like one another. The King of Prussia would say: 'George is the uncle of Frederick, but George is not the uncle of the King of Prussia.' Finally he told me: 'Let France declare war on England, and I will march off to battle.'

This was all I needed. I quickly returned to the French court: I reported on my trip. I transmitted the hopes that had been raised in Berlin. These hopes were not deceptive; and the following spring, the King of Prussia did indeed draw up a new treatise with the King of France. He advanced into Bohemia with one hundred thousand men, while the Austrians were in Alsace.

If I had recounted my adventures to any worthy Parisian, and the services I had rendered, he would have been in no doubt that I would be promoted to some office of distinction. This was my reward:

The Duchesse de Châteauroux was annoyed that the negotiations had not been held with her as a direct inter-mediary; she had decided that she wished to get rid of M. Amelot, since he had a stammer and this minor defect irritated her; in addition, she hated this same Amelot because he took his orders from M. de Maurepas; he was dismissed within a week, and I was dragged down with him.

It happened a short time afterwards that Louis XV fell gravely ill in the city of Metz: M. de Maurepas and his cabal used this occasion to destroy Mme de Châteauroux. The Bishop of Soissons, Fitz-James, the son of the bastard of James II, regarded as a saint, decided that it was his duty as first chaplain to try and convert the King, and declared to him that he would give him neither absolution nor communion unless he dismissed his mistress and her sister, the Duchesse de Lauraguais, and their friends. The two sisters departed, bearing with them the curses of the people of Metz. It was for this action that the people of Paris, just as foolish as the people of Metz, gave Louis XV the nickname of *the Beloved*. A rascal named Vadé dreamt up this title, and the broadsheets spread it around. When this prince recovered, his only wish was to be the beloved of his mistress. They were more in love than ever. She was to return to her ministry; she was about to leave Paris for Versailles when she died suddenly as a result of the rage that her dismissal had caused her. She was soon forgotten.

A mistress was needed. The choice fell on a certain lady named Poisson, the daughter of a kept woman and a peasant from La Ferté-sous-Jouarre, who had amassed his wealth by selling corn to suppliers of food.[39] This poor man was on the run at the time, having been sentenced for embezzlement. His daughter had been married off to the under-farmer Le Normand, lord of Etiolles, nephew of the farmer general Le Normand de Tournehem, the lover of her mother. The daughter was well brought up, sensible, likeable, graceful and talented, having been born with common sense and a kind heart. I knew her quite well; I was even the confidant of her love. She admitted to me that she had always had a present-iment that she would be loved by the King, and that she had felt an overwhelming attraction for him, without really seeking to understand why.

This idea, which might well have seemed perfectly illusory given her situation, was based on the fact that she had often been taken to watch the King hunting in the forest of Sénart. Tournehem, her mother's lover, had a country house nearby. Madame d'Etiolles was driven along in a fine calash. The King noticed her, and often sent her roe deer. Her mother kept telling him that she was prettier than Mme de Châteauroux, and old Tournehem kept exclaiming: 'There's no denying that Madame Poisson's daughter is fit for a king!' Finally, when she had held the King in her arms, she told me that she firmly believed in destiny; and she was right. I spent a few months in Etiolles with her, while the King was embarked on his 1746 campaign.

This earned me rewards that I had never before received, either for the services I had rendered or the works I had written. I was judged worthy to be one of the forty useless members of the Academy. I was appointed Historiographer of France; and the King presented me with a position as a gentleman ordinary of his bedchamber. I concluded that if one wishes to make even the smallest fortune, it is better to say a few words to a King's mistress than to write a hundred tomes.

As soon as I started to look pleased with my lot, all my colleagues, the wits of Paris, unleashed against me all the remorseless animosity that they were bound to feel for someone who had won all the prizes they themselves deserved.

I was still bound to the Marquise du Châtelet by the most unswerving friendship and by our shared taste for study. We would spend time together in Paris and the countryside. Cirey is on the borders of the Lorraine region: at that time, King Stanislas was holding his small and agreeable court at Lunéville.[40] Although he was old and devout, he had a mistress, Mme la Marquise de Boufflers. He shared his soul between her and a Jesuit by the name of Menou; of all the priests I have ever known, he was the one most deeply involved in bold and cunning intrigues. This man had picked up about a million from the King; the latter's wife, who was ruled by Menou, had importuned her husband for this favour. Part of the money was used to build a magnificent house for him and several other Jesuits in the city of Nancy. This house brought in an income of twenty-four thousand pounds: twelve for Menou's table, and twelve to give to whomever he wished.

The mistress was not so well treated – far from it. She barely got enough money from the King of Poland to buy herself dresses; and yet the Jesuit envied her portion, and was furiously jealous of the Marquise. They had openly quarrelled. Every day, the King found it extremely difficult, after Mass, to reconcile his mistress and his confessor.

Finally our Jesuit, having heard about Mme du Châtelet, who had a nice figure and was still rather attractive, decided he would use her to replace Mme de Boufflers. Stanislas sometimes took it into his head to produce some rather mediocre writings: Menou believed that a woman who was an author would manage more easily than another to find favour with him. So along he came to Cirey to hatch this cunning plot: he cajoled Mme du Châtelet, and told us that King Stanislas would be delighted to see us. He returned to tell the King that we were burning with the desire to pay court to him; Stanislas requested Mme de Boufflers to bring us along.

And so we did indeed spend the whole of the year 1749 in Lunéville. Things turned out completely differently from what the Reverend Father had hoped for. We became close to Mme de Boufflers; and the Jesuit now had two women to contend with.

Life at the Court of Lorraine was quite pleasant, although there were, here as elsewhere, intrigues and vexatious gossip. Poncet, the Bishop of Troyes, suffering from debt and a poor reputation, tried at the end of the year to swell the number of our court and add to our vexations. (When I say he had a poor reputation, I also have in mind the poor reputation enjoyed by his funeral orations and his sermons.) By means of our ladies, he managed to be appointed to the post of Grand Chaplain of the King, who was flattered to have a bishop on his payroll – not that he was paid very much.

This Bishop did not arrive until 1750. He started off by falling in love with Mme de Boufflers, and was dismissed. His anger fell on Louis XV, Stanislas' son-in-law: for on his return to Troyes, he tried to play a role in the ridiculous business of the confession notes invented by the Archbishop of Paris, Beaumont;[41] he held firm against the *Parlement*, and defied the King. This was no way of paying off his debts; but it was a way of getting himself thrown into jail. The King of France sent him off to be locked away in Alsace, in a monastery filled with fat German monks. But I must return to my own story.

Madame du Châtelet died in Stanislas' palace, after an illness of two days. We were all so distressed that none of us even thought of summoning a priest, a Jesuit or the sacraments. She did not have to endure the full horrors of death; only we experienced them. I was overwhelmed by a sense of utter devastation. The kindly King Stanislas came to my room to comfort me and shed tears with me. Few of his fellow kings do as much in such circumstances. He wished me to stay: I could not stand Lunéville any longer, and I returned to Paris.

It was my fate to go from one King to another, although I was devoted to and indeed passionately fond of my freedom. The King of Prussia, to whom I had often intimated that I would never leave Mme du Châtelet for him, did his utmost to catch me now that he was rid of his rival. At that time he was enjoying a period of peace that he had won through his victories, and his leisure time was always employed in writing poetry, or composing the history of his country and his campaigns. He was perfectly convinced, if truth be told, that his poetry and his prose were far better than my prose and my poetry, as far as the content was concerned; but he believed that when it came to the form, I would be able, as an Academician, to give his writings a certain polish; there was no seductive flattery that he failed to employ in order to persuade me to come.

How could I resist a victorious king who was also a poet, musician and philosopher, and who claimed to love me? I thought that I loved him too. Eventually I set off for Potsdam in the month of June 1750. I was given a warmer welcome than Astolfo in the palace of Alcina.[42] To be housed in the apartment that had belonged to the Maréchal de Saxe, to have at my disposal the King's chefs when I wished to eat at home, and his coachmen when I wished to go out: these were the least of the favours that were showered on me. The dinners were most enjoyable. I do not know whether I am mistaken, but it seems to me that they were the scene of much witty talk; the King was witty and made others witty too; and the most extraordinary thing is that I have never enjoyed such relaxed mealtimes. I would work with His Majesty for two hours a day; I corrected all his works, never failing to praise to the skies whatever was good in them, while crossing out all the bad bits. I explained everything in writing to him, and this comprised a rhetoric and a poetics for his own use; he benefited from this, and his genius served him even better than did my lessons. I did not need to pay court to anyone, nor to pay anyone a visit or fulfil any duties. I had created a life of freedom for myself, and I could conceive of nothing more agreeable than such a state.

Alcina-Frederick, who could see that my head was already quite turned, redoubled his magic potions to intoxicate me completely. The final act of seduction was a letter that he wrote from his apartment to me in mine. A mistress expresses her feelings no more tenderly; he endeavoured in this letter to dissipate the fear that his rank and his character inspired in me; it included these strange words:

How could I ever be the occasion of misfortune to a man whom I esteem, whom I love, and who is sacrificing to me his native land and all that humankind counts most dear?... I respect you as my master in eloquence. I love you as a virtuous friend. What slavery, what mishap, what alteration is there to fear in a land where you are esteemed as much as you are in your own country, and at the home of a friend whose heart is filled with gratitude? I respected the friendship that bound you to Mme du Châtelet; but, after her, I was one of your oldest friends. I promise you that you will be happy here for as long as my life shall last.

This is the kind of letter few majesties ever write. It was the last drop of potion and it filled my cup to overflowing. His spoken expressions of affection were even stronger than the written ones. He was accustomed to making singular demonstrations of affection towards favourites who were younger than myself; and, forgetting for a moment that I was not their age, and that I did not have a pretty hand, he seized mine to kiss it. I kissed his in turn, and made myself his slave. Permission was needed from the King of France to belong to two masters. The King of Prussia promised to do everything necessary.

He wrote to ask the King my master if he would give me away. I had never imagined that anyone at Versailles would be shocked by a gentleman ordinary of the bedchamber, which is the most useless species at Court, becoming a useless chamberlain at Berlin. I was given full permission. But this was accompanied by a certain resentment, and I was not forgiven. I greatly displeased the King of France, without pleasing the King of Prussia – who, deep down, did not much care what happened to me.

So there I was, with a key of silver gilt hanging on my jacket, the cross of my decoration round my neck and a pension of twenty thousand francs. Maupertuis was sick with jealousy, and I did not even notice. At that time, there was in Berlin a doctor called La Mettrie,[43] the most brazen atheist in all the Faculties of Medicine in Europe: besides this, he was a merry, pleasant, scatterbrained man, as well versed in theory as any of his colleagues, and, incontestably, the worst doctor in the world when it came to practice; in fact, thank God, he did not practise. He had mocked the entire Faculty of Medicine in Paris, and had even produced many scurrilous and personal writings against the doctors, who did not forgive him; they obtained a decree ordering him to be apprehended. So La Mettrie had withdrawn to Berlin, where his gaiety rather amused people; he also wrote, and published, the most outrageous things on ethics that you can imagine. His books pleased the King, who made him, not his doctor, but his reader.

One day, after he had read to the King, La Mettrie (who would say to the King the first thing that he thought of) told him people were really jealous of my favour and my good fortune. 'Leave them to it,' replied the King, 'oranges are to be squeezed: after you have swallowed the juice, you throw the orange away.' La Mettrie did not fail to report to me this fine aphorism, worthy of Dionysius of Syracuse.[44]

At this juncture I decided to put the orange peel in a safe place. I had some three hundred thousand pounds to invest. Naturally, I refrained from placing these funds in the States of my Alcina; I invested them very advantageously in some land which the Duke of Württemberg possesses in France. The King, who opened all my letters, started to suspect that I was not intending to stay with him. However, the mania for writing poetry possessed him as much as it had Dionysius. I was forever labouring away, polishing his style, revising yet again his *History of Brandenburg* and everything he composed.

La Mettrie died at the home of Milord Tyrconnel, the French envoy, at which he ate a whole *pâté aux truffes*, after a very long dinner. It was claimed that he had been given confession before dying; the King was most indignant: he made close inquiries to find out if this was true; he was assured that it was a most dreadful slander, and that La Mettrie had died as he had lived, rejecting God and his doctors. His Majesty, fully satisfied, immediately composed his funeral oration, which he had read in his name at the public sitting of the Academy by his secretary Darget, and he gave a pension of six hundred pounds to a prostitute whom La Mettrie had brought with him from Paris when he had abandoned his wife and children.

Maupertuis, who knew the anecdote about the orange peel, waited a while before spreading the rumour that I had said that the post of King's Atheist was now vacant. This slander did not gain any credence; but he added, on top of this, that I thought the King's poetry was no good – and this story was believed.

I noticed that from that time onward, the King's suppers were not so merry; I was given less poetry to correct; my disgrace was total.

Algarotti, Darget and another Frenchman named Chasot, who was one of his finest officers, all left him at the same time. I was preparing to do the same. But before I did, I wished to give myself the pleasure of making fun of a book that Maupertuis had just published. It was a golden opportunity; nobody had ever written anything so ridiculous and crazy. The fellow was seriously proposing to undertake a journey straight to the two poles; to dissect the heads of giants, so as to find out what their souls were like by examining their brains; to build a city where the only language spoken would be Latin; to dig a hole to the very centre of the earth; to cure illnesses by coating the patients with resin; and finally to predict the future by going into ecstasy.[45]

The King laughed at the book, I laughed at it, everybody laughed at it. But then a rather more serious scene occurred in connection with some silly, dull piece of mathematics that Maupertuis wished to set up as a discovery. A more knowledge-able geometer, named König, the librarian of the Princess of Orange at The Hague, pointed out Maupertuis's errors to him, and told him that Leibniz, who had previously examined this old idea, had demonstrated that it was false in several letters, of which he showed him copies.[46]

Maupertuis, President of the Academy of Berlin, was angry that a foreign associate should prove to him that he had blundered, and firstly persuaded the King that König, as a man established in Holland, was his enemy, and had made some very negative comments about His Majesty's prose and poetry to the Princess of Orange.

Having taken this first precaution, he got a few poor pensionaries of the Academy, who were dependent on him, to have König condemned as a forger and struck off the list of Academicians. The geometer of Holland had anticipated this, and had sent back the letters patent that conferred on him the dignity of a member of the Berlin Academy.

All the writers in Europe were as indignant at Maupertuis's manoeuvres as they were irritated by his dreary book. He drew down on himself the hatred and contempt of those who prided themselves on understanding philosophy as well as those who did not know a thing about it. In Berlin, people contented themselves with a shrug, since, as the King had taken sides in this unhappy business, nobody dared to say anything; I was the only person to speak out. König was my friend; I simultaneously enjoyed the pleasure of defending the freedom of writers by supporting a friend, and that of mortifying an enemy – a man who was an enemy of modesty as much as he was an enemy of mine. I had no plans to stay in Berlin; I have always preferred liberty above everything else. Few writers can say the same. Most of them are poor; poverty wears down one's courage; and every philosopher at Court becomes as much of a slave as the first officer of the Crown. I felt how greatly my liberty must displease a king who was more absolute than the Great Turk. He was a funny kind of a king in his own home, it has to be admitted. He protected Maupertuis, and mocked him more than anyone else did. He started to write against him, and sent his manuscript to me in my rooms, delivered by one of the ministers of his secret pleasures called Marwitz; he scoffed at the idea of the hole at the earth's centre, his method of curing people with a coating of resin, his voyage to the south pole, the Latin-speaking city, and the cowardice of his Academy, which had suffered in silence the tyranny exercised against poor König. But, as his motto was 'No noise unless I make it myself', he had everything that had been written on this subject burnt, except for his own work.

I sent back to him the decoration he had given me, his chamberlain's key, and his pensions; then he did everything he could to keep me there, and I did everything I could to leave him. He gave me back his cross and his key, and re-quested that I dine with him; so I sat through yet another meal of Damocles; whereupon I left, promising to return, but firmly resolved never to see him again for as long as I lived.

Thus there were four of us who made our escape within the same short period: Chasot, Darget, Algarotti and myself. Indeed, there was no way we could have stayed on. Everyone knows that you have to suffer indignities from kings; but Frederick was abusing his prerogative just a little too much. Society has its laws, unless it is the society of the lion and the goat. Frederick always failed to observe the first law of society: say nothing disobliging to anyone. He would often ask his chamberlain Pöllnitz if he would not be glad to change religion for the fourth time, and he offered to pay a hundred *écus* in ready money for his conversion. 'Good Lord, my dear Pöllnitz!' he would say, 'I have forgotten the name of that man whom you robbed in The Hague, when you sold him fake silver as fine silver; do please help me remember, I beg you.' He treated poor d'Argens in a rather similar way. All the same, these two victims stayed on. Pöllnitz, who had squandered all his wealth, was obliged to swallow all these insults just to live; it was the only way he could earn his bread; and d'Argens possessed nothing else in the world but his *Jewish Letters*, together with his wife, Cochois by name, an untalented provincial actress so ugly that she could never succeed in any trade, even though she tried several. As for Maupertuis, who had been so ill advised as to bring all his wealth with him to Berlin, he did not reflect that it is better to have a hundred *pistoles* in a free country than a thousand in a despotic country, and he was forced to languish in the chains that he himself had forged.

On leaving my Alcina's palace, I went to spend a month with the Duchess of Saxe-Gotha, the best princess in the world, the gentlest, wisest and most even-tempered – and one who, thank God, did not write poetry. From thence I went for a few days to the country house of the Landgrave of Hesse, who was even less interested in poetry than the Princess of Gotha. I could breathe freely. I slowly made my way on, via Frankfurt. It was here that the most bizarre destiny awaited me.

I fell ill in Frankfurt; one of my nieces, the widow of a captain in the regiment of Champagne, a very pleasant woman of many talents, and who in addition was regarded in Paris as good company, was bold enough to leave Paris and come and meet me on the Main; but she found that I had been made a prisoner of war. This is how this fine turn of events had occurred. There was in Frankfurt a certain Freytag, banished from Dresden, where he had been forced to wear an iron collar and sentenced to hard labour. He had since become an agent of the King of Prussia in Frankfurt. The King liked to use ministers such as this, since the only wages they earned were whatever they could pick up from innocent passers-by.

This ambassador and a merchant by the name of Schmid, who had previously been fined for counterfeiting money, intimated to me, on behalf of His Majesty the King of Prussia, that I would not be able to leave Frankfurt until I had given back the valuables that I had brought away from His Majesty. 'Alas, gentlemen! I have brought nothing away from that country, I swear to you – not even the least regret for leaving. So what are those jewels in the Crown of Brandenburg that you want me to hand back?'

'It vas, Mossieur,' replied Freytag, 'the vork of pohetry of my gracious master the King.'

'Oh! I'm only too happy to give him back his prose and his poetry,' I replied, 'although, after all, I have more than one claim on the work. He presented me with a fine copy of it, printed at his own expense. Unfortunately, this copy is in Leipzig with all my other things.' Then Freytag suggested that I stay in Frankfurt until the treasure had arrived from Leipzig; and he signed this fine note for me:

Mossieur, as soon as the big bundle from Leipzig is here, containing the vork of pohetry *of my master the King, which His Majesty requires, and the* vork of pohetry *is returned to me, you will be able to leave for wherever you wish.*

Frankfurt, 1st June 1753.
FREYTAG, *resident of my master the King.*

At the bottom of the note I wrote: *I.O.U. the vork of pohetry of the King your master*: at which the resident was most satisfied.

On 17th June the big bundle of *pohetry* arrived. I faithfully handed over this sacred package entrusted to my care, and I thought I would now be able to leave without failing in my duty to any crowned head; but just as I was leaving, I was arrested, together with my secretary and my servants; my niece was arrested; four soldiers dragged her through the mud to the house of the merchant Schmid, who had some title or other as a privy councillor to the King of Prussia. This Frankfurt merchant thought himself to be a Prussian general: he commanded twelve soldiers of the city in this highly significant affair, with all the self-importance and hauteur required. My niece had a passport authorised by the King of France, and she had never corrected the poetry of the King of Prussia. Usually, ladies are shown respect even in the horrors of war; but councillor Schmid and resident Freytag, in acting on behalf of Frederick, thought they would pay court to him by dragging the gentle sex through the mud.

We were all shoved into a kind of hostelry, at the door of which twelve soldiers were posted: four others were placed in my room, four in an attic to which my niece had been taken, and four in a garret open to the four winds, where my secretary was forced to sleep on straw. My niece did in fact have a little bed; but her four soldiers, with their bayonets fixed, acted as her curtains and her chambermaids.

However much we repeated that we would appeal to Caesar, that the Emperor had been elected in Frankfurt, that my secretary was a Florentine and a subject of His Imperial Majesty, that my niece and I were subjects of the Most Christian King, and that we had no bone to pick with the Margrave of Brandenburg,[47] we were told in reply that the Margrave had more credit in Frankfurt than did the Emperor. We were kept prisoners of this war for twelve days, and we were obliged to pay a hundred and forty *écus* per day.

The merchant Schmid had seized all of my belongings, which were handed back to me half as light as they had been before. No higher price could have been paid for the *vork of pohetry of the King of Prussia*. I lost roughly the same sum of money as he had spent to persuade me to go and give him lessons. So now we were quits.

To complete the adventure, a certain Van Duren, a bookseller in The Hague, a scoundrel by profession and a fraudulent bankrupt by habit, was living in retirement in Frankfurt. This was the same man to whom, thirteen years previously, I had presented the manuscript of Frederick's *Anti-Machiavelli*. You can always count on running into your friends just when you need them. He claimed that His Majesty owed him twenty ducats or so, and that I was responsible for paying them back. He included interest, and interest on the interest. Master Fichard, bourgmestre of Frankfurt, and indeed the reigning bourgmestre, as they say, found – in his capacity as bourgmestre – that the account was correct, and – in his capacity as reigning – he forced me to disburse thirty ducats, took twenty-six for himself and gave four to that rascal the bookseller.

Now this whole business of Ostrogoths and Vandals was concluded, I embraced my hosts, and thanked them for their kindly welcome.

Some time later, I went to take the waters at Plombières; I drank especially deeply of those of Lethe, fully convinced that misfortunes, of whatever kind, are good for nothing except to be forgotten. My niece, Mme Denis, who was the consolation of my life, and who had grown close to me thanks to her taste for letters and to her most tender friendship, accompanied me from Plombières to Lyons. Here I was given a tumultuous welcome by the whole of the city, and a rather chillier welcome by the Cardinal de Tencin, Archbishop of Lyons, so notorious for the way he had made his fortune by making a Catholic of that Law or Lass, the author of the System which wrought such havoc in France.[48] His council of Embrun completed the fortune which Law's conversion had begun. The System made him so rich that he had enough to buy a cardinal's hat. He was Minister of State; and in his capacity as a minister, he admitted to me privately that he could not invite me to dinner in public, because the King of France was cross with me for leaving him for the King of Prussia. I told him that I never ate dinner, and that, as far as kings were concerned, I was more able to cope with their whims than anyone else in the world, and the same went for cardinals. I had been recommended to try the waters of Aix in Savoy; although they were under the dominion of a king, I set off to go and taste them. I had to pass via Geneva: the celebrated doctor Tronchin, who had established himself in Geneva shortly before, declared to me that the waters of Aix would kill me, and that he would make me live.

I accepted his proposal. No Catholic is allowed to settle in Geneva, nor in the Protestant cantons of Switzerland. It struck me as amusing that I would be acquiring land in the only countries on earth where I was not permitted to own any.

I purchased, by a strange deal for which there was no precedent in that country, a small piece of land some sixty acres in size, which was sold to me for twice the price that it would have cost me in the environs of Paris; but pleasure never comes too dear; the house is attractive and comfortable; it is in a fine setting; one is astonished at its charm, and never wearies of it. On one side lies Lake Geneva, and on the other the city. The Rhone comes foaming out and forms a channel at the bottom of my garden; the River Arve, coming down from

Savoy, flows swiftly into the Rhone; further on, you can see yet another river. A hundred country houses, a hundred bright gardens, adorn the sides of the lake and the rivers; in the distance, the Alps rise up and, between their peaks, you can make out twenty leagues of mountains, covered with eternal snow. I have an even more beautiful house and a more extens-ive view in Lausanne; but my house near Geneva is much more agreeable. In these two dwelling-places I have what kings never give, or rather what they deprive one of: peace and liberty; and I also have what they sometimes give, and which I do not need to obtain from them; I put into practice what I said in *The Worldling*:

Oh, what a grand time is this Age of Iron![49]

All the comforts of life – in furnishings, retinue and good food – can be found in my two houses; a pleasant company, including several wits, fills the moments left over from studying and looking after my health. There is enough here to make more than one of my dear fellow writers burst with envy: yet I was not born rich, far from it. People ask me by what art I have managed to live like a farmer general; it is a good idea to say how, so that I may serve as an example. I have seen so many writers poor and scorned, and so I concluded long ago that I would not increase their number.

In France, one must be either an anvil or a hammer: I was born an anvil. A small patrimony shrinks every day, because everything increases in price over the long term, and often the government has interfered with one's income and the cur-rency. One needs to pay close attention to all the interventions which the minister, always in debt and always changing tack, makes in State finances. There is always one such operation by which an individual can profit, without being obliged to anyone; and nothing is so sweet as to make one's fortune by oneself: the first step costs a few painful efforts; the others are easy. You need to be thrifty in your youth; in old age, you find you have built up a rather surprising amount. This is the age at which a fortune is most essential; it is the age which I am at present enjoying; and, having lived at the courts of kings, I have made myself king in my own home, in spite of immense losses.

Since I have been living in this peaceful opulence, and in the most absolute independence, the King of Prussia has come back to me; in 1755, he sent me an opera which he composed, based on my tragedy *Mérope*: it is without any argument the worst thing he has ever done. Since then he has continued to write to me; I have always maintained a correspondence with his sister the Margravine of Bayreuth, who has kept up her unswerving kindness to me.

While I was in my retreat enjoying the sweetest life imaginable, I had the small philosophical pleasure of seeing that the kings of Europe were not able to enjoy this same happy tranquillity, and of concluding that the situation of a private individual is often preferable to that of the greatest monarchs, as you shall see.

England waged a piratical war on France, over a few acres of snow, in 1756;[50] at the same time, the Empress, Queen of Hungary, seemed to have something of a desire to take back, if she could, her dear Silesia, which the King of Prussia had stolen from her. To this end she entered on negotiations with the Empress of Russia and with the King of Poland, though merely in his capacity as Elector of Saxony: for nobody negotiates with the Poles. The King of France, on his side, wanted to take revenge on the States of Hanover for the damage which the Elector of Hanover, the King of England, was causing him by sea. Frederick, who was at this time allied with France, and who was profoundly contemptuous of our government, preferred to forge an alliance with England rather than France, and joined up with the House of Hanover, expecting that with one hand he would be able to prevent the Russians from advancing into his Prussia, and with the other stop the French from coming into Germany: he was wrong on both counts; but he had a third plan, and here he was not in the least mistaken: he wanted to invade Saxony on the pretext of friendship, and to wage war on the Empress, Queen of Hungary, with the money he pillaged from the Saxons.

The Marquis of Brandenburg, by this strange manoeuvre, changed the whole system of Europe single-handedly. The King of France, wishing to keep him in the alliance, had sent him the Duc de Nivernois, an intelligent man, who wrote very agreeable poetry. The embassy of a duke and peer and of a poet seemed designed to flatter the vanity and taste of Frederick; he scorned the King of France, and signed his treaty with England on the very same day that the ambassador arrived in Berlin, politely played cat and mouse with the duke and peer, and wrote an epigram on the poet.

In those days it was the privilege of poetry to govern states. There was another poet in Paris, a man of breeding, very poor but very likeable – in a word, the Abbé de Bernis, who later became a cardinal. He had started by writing poetry against me, and had later become my friend, which was of not the slightest use to him; but he had also become the friend of Mme de Pompadour – which was rather more useful. He had been sent from Parnassus on an embassy to Venice; he was then in Paris, where he enjoyed great credit.

The King of Prussia, in that fine book of *pohetry* that M. Freytag had asked for so insistently in Frankfurt, had slipped in a line aimed against the Abbé de Bernis.

Avoid the sterile facility of the Abbé de Bernis.

I do not think that this book and this line of poetry had reached the Abbé; but, as God is just, God used him to avenge France on the King of Prussia. The Abbé drew up an offensive and defensive treaty with M. de Stahremberg, the Austrian ambassador, in spite of Rouillé, who was then Minister of Foreign Affairs. Madame de Pompadour presided over these negotiations: Rouillé was obliged to sign the treaty conjointly with the Abbé de Bernis, which was unprecedented. This Minister Rouillé, it has to be admitted, was the most inept Secretary of State that a king of France had ever had, and the most ignorant pedant to wear a gown. One day he had asked whether Veteravia was in Italy.[51] So long as there was nothing too tricky to deal with, he was tolerated; but as soon as serious matters arose, his inadequacy made itself felt, he was dismissed, and the Abbé de Bernis took his place.

Mademoiselle Poisson, Mme Le Normand, Marquise de Pompadour, was really the first minister of State. Certain highly insulting words aimed against her by Frederick, who never spared either women or poets, had wounded the heart of the Marquise, and contributed in no small degree to that revolution in human affairs that, at a stroke, united the houses of France and Austria, after over two hundred years of a hatred that was considered to be immortal. The Court of France, which in 1741 had thought it could crush Austria, in 1756 supported it, and eventually we saw France, Russia, Sweden, Hungary, half of Germany and the fiscal of the Empire all declaring against one man: the Marquis of Brandenburg.

This prince, whose grandfather had barely been able to keep up twenty thousand men, had an army of one hundred thousand infantry and forty thousand cavalry, well organised, even better exercised and provided with everything it needed; but still, there were over four hundred thousand soldiers arrayed against Brandenburg.

It turned out that, in this war, each party first seized what it could lay its hands on. Frederick took Saxony, France took the States of Frederick from the city of Guelders to Minden on the Weser, and for a while seized the whole Electorate of Hanover and Hesse, which was allied with Frederick; the Empress of Russia took all of Prussia: this king, at first beaten by the Russians, beat the Austrians, and was then beaten by them in Bohemia on 18th June 1757.[52]

The loss of a battle seemed bound to crush this monarch; harried on all sides by the Russians, the Austrians and France, he thought he was lost. The Maréchal de Richelieu had just concluded, near Stade, a treaty with the Hanoverians and the Hessians which resembled that of the Caudine Forks.[53] Their army was no longer to serve; the Maréchal was ready to enter Saxony with sixty thousand men; the Prince de Soubise was about to enter it from the other side with over thirty thousand, and was supported by the army of the Circles of the Empire;[54] from there, they marched on Berlin. The Austrians had won a second engagement, and were already in Breslau; one of their generals had even made a dash to Berlin and had appropriated some of its wealth; the treasury of the King of Prussia had been almost emptied, and soon not a village would be left him; he would be outlawed by the Empire; his trial had begun; he was declared a rebel; and, if he were captured, there was every likelihood that he would be sentenced to lose his head.

In these extremities, the idea of killing himself passed through his mind. He wrote to his sister, the Margravine of Bayreuth, that he was going to end his life: he did not want to end the drama without a few lines of poetry; the passion for poetry was still stronger in him than hatred of life. So he wrote to the Marquis d'Argens a long verse epistle, in which he explained his decision, and bade him farewell. However strange this epistle may seem, both because of its subject matter and because of the man who wrote it (as well as because of its addressee), it is not possible to copy it all out here, as it is so repetitive; but in it you find a few passages that are, for a king from the North, quite nicely turned; here are a few excerpts:

> *The die is cast, my friend:*
> *My pain and grief will soon be at an end;*
> *I have been crushed under misfortune's yoke*
> *And plan to end my suffering at a stroke.*
> *Nature has burdened me with nought but sorrow:*
> *Tomorrow and tomorrow and tomorrow…*
> *No more; but, brave of heart and firm of gaze,*
> *I boldly stride towards my end of days*
> *To quiet all the heartache that they bring,*
> > *And cease without a pain.*
> > *Farewell: I have been King;*
> > *Farewell: it was a dream.*
> *Those quickly fading flowers will never again*
> > *Dazzle my weary eyes.*
> > *My early morning skies*
> > *Gleamed with such wild desires*
> *Of pleasure and joy… but they are long since past,*
> > *And Zeno's stern philosophy*
> > *Has cured me of frivolity*
> *And all life's daydreams have been laid to rest.*
> > *Farewell, all joy and bliss;*
> > *Farewell, all pleasures of the flesh*

That bind us with your flowery chains…
But, crushed beneath my pains,
Great God, what empty names
To me are 'cheer' and 'jolliness'!
Caught within the vulture's grip
Can the tender turtle dove,
The plaintive Philomel,[55]
Breathe a single word of love?
The radiant sun above
For too long now has shone down on my hell
And Morpheus has withheld his poppies
From weary eyes that cannot sleep.
The morning I would greet with sobs and tears:
    'The day will soon be here:
    It fills me with fresh fear.'
When night returned, I'd murmur with a groan:
    'Ah, here you are again,
    Eternalising pain.'

Heroes of liberty! You whom I revere!
Oh shade of Cato, shade of Brutus dear![56]
    Your example I will follow:
    Lead me from this maze of sorrow –
Light me with the bright torch of your death,
Far from the madding crowd show me the way
Your ancient virtue can still lead to truth…
I scorn the fairy tales and gloomy ghosts
That Superstition plants within men's breasts.
If I'm to know what we men really are,
I'll keep Religion and its lures at bay.
    My master Epicurus!
    Of those illusions cure us!

All compound things are subject to decay
By time's erosion, as you truly say;
    This breath, this spark within us,
    This vivifying fire,
Is just as mortal as all creatures are:
It's born into our bodies when we're born,
Waxes and wanes from childhood to old age,
Suffers from all life's cruelty and pain
And stumbles on its way to dreary dotage.
Surely it will also perish when the evening
Closes our eyes and leads us from the living.
    I wander, vanquished and alone
    Across this world, betrayed by 'friends'
    (Or rather heartless foes)
    And suffer far more woes
In this drear world than, as the fables tell,
    Prometheus bore in hell.[57]
And so, to put an end to all these pains,
I'll imitate those wretched prisoners
Who, cheating their cruel jailors
At last break off their chains.
    I pay no heed to how:
    The time to go is now.
    I snap the dreadful bonds
    That tied my soul too long
    To this poor body crushed by grief and pain.
    Here lies the cause of my self-chosen doom.
    In this dark, empty room
        I do not hope for
        Apotheosis –
    But when spring comes again
    And buds begin to flower,

Remember me. With myrtles and with roses
   Adorn my tomb.

He sent me this epistle written by his hand. There are several half-lines pillaged from the Abbé de Chaulieu and myself. The ideas are incoherent, the poetry in general inelegant, but there are some good lines; and it is a great deal for a king to write an epistle of two hundred clumsy lines of verse, given the state he was in. He wanted it to be said that he had preserved all his presence and freedom of mind at a time when they are generally lacking in a man.

The letter he wrote to me expressed the same feelings; but there were fewer myrtles and roses, and less of Ixion and his deep grief.[58] I used prose to combat the decision to die that he claimed he had taken, and I had no difficulty in persuading him to live. I advised him to embark on negotiations with the Maréchal de Richelieu, and to imitate the Duke of Cumberland;[59] in a word I took all the liberties that one can take with a despairing poet, who was on the verge of ceasing to be a king. He did indeed write to the Maréchal de Richelieu; but when he received no reply, he resolved to beat us. He informed me that he was going to fight the Prince de Soubise; his letter finished with some lines of verse that were worthier of his situation, his dignity, his courage and his spirit:

When the storm's about to break,
Threatening you with imminent shipwreck,
Then think, and live, and die just like a king.

As he marched against the French and the Imperial troops, he wrote to the Margravine of Bayreuth, his sister, to say that he would be killed; but he was more fortunate than he said and believed. On 5th November 1757 he awaited the French and Imperial army at a rather advantageous position, Rossbach, on the borders of Saxony; and, as he had always been saying he would get killed, he requested his brother, Prince Henry, to fulfil his promise at the head of five Prussian battalions that were meant to withstand the first attacks launched by the enemy armies, while his artillery would pound them and his cavalry would attack theirs.

Indeed, Prince Henry sustained a light rifle wound to his throat; and he was, I believe, the only Prussian to be wounded on this day. The French and the Austrians fled at the first volley. It was the most unprecedented and the most complete rout in the annals of history. This Battle of Rossbach will be celebrated for a long time. Thirty thousand Frenchmen and twenty thousand Imperial soldiers took to a shameful and headlong flight before five battalions and a few squadrons. The defeats of Agincourt, Crécy and Poitiers were not so humiliating.

The discipline and drilling that his father had established, and which the son had intensified, were the real reason for this strange victory. Prussian drilling had improved considerably over the last fifty years. People had tried to imitate it in France as in every other State; but it had been impossible to accomplish in three or four years, with French soldiers who were less amenable to discipline, what had been done with the Prussians in fifty. Indeed, in France, the manoeuvres had been changed at practically every review; as a result, the officers and soldiers, having failed properly to learn the new drills – all of them different – had learned nothing at all, and really had no discipline and no training. In a word, at the mere sight of the Prussians, they turned and fled in panic, and fortune brought Frederick, in a quarter of an hour, from the depths of despair to the pinnacle of success and glory.

However, he was afraid that this success would be very fleeting; he was afraid he would have to stand up to the combined might of the powers of France, Russia and Austria, and he would very much have liked to separate Louis XV from Maria Theresa.

The ill-starred battle of Rossbach made the whole of France murmur against the treaty the Abbé de Bernis had concluded with the court of Vienna. The Cardinal de Tencin, Archbishop of Lyons, had kept his rank as a minister of State, and a private correspondence with the King of France; he, more than anyone, was opposed to the alliance with the Austrian court. When I had gone to Lyons, he had given me a reception that he must have thought would leave me aggrieved; but the desire to involve oneself in intrigues that had followed him into retirement, and – so people claim – never abandons men of rank, led him to join forces with me in an attempt to engage the Margravine of Bayreuth to place herself in his hands and entrust the interests of the King her brother to him. He wished to reconcile the King of Prussia with the King of France, and thought he could procure peace. It was not very difficult to bring the Margravine of Bayreuth and the King her brother round to negotiating on this matter; I took the task upon myself with all the more pleasure in that I could see perfectly well it would not succeed.

The Margravine of Bayreuth wrote on behalf of the King her brother. Letters between this princess and the Cardinal passed through my hands: I had the secret satisfaction of being the pimp to the whole great business, as well as another pleasure, perhaps, that of sensing that my Cardinal was heading for a terrible fall. He wrote an eloquent letter to the King, attaching the Margravine's letter to it; but he was quite astonished when the King replied rather curtly that the

Secretary of State for Foreign Affairs would inform him of his intentions.

Indeed, the Abbé de Bernis dictated to the Cardinal the answer he was to give: this answer was a downright refusal to enter into negotiations. He was obliged to sign the model of the letter which the Abbé de Bernis had sent him; he sent me this letter, which put an end to all his hopes, and died of pique a fortnight later.

I have never understood how anyone can die of pique, and how ministers and old cardinals, who are so hard-hearted, still have enough sensibility to be dealt a mortal blow over a minor setback: I had intended to make fun of him, to mortify him and not to kill him.

There was a kind of grandeur in the way the ministry of France refused to make peace with the King of Prussia, after having been beaten and humiliated by him; there was good faith and a good deal of kindness in the way it sacrificed itself for the House of Austria as well: for a long time these virtues were not properly rewarded by Fortune.

The powers of Hanover, Brunswick and Hesse were less faithful to their treaties, and did better as a result. They had stipulated with the Maréchal de Richelieu that they would no longer serve against us, and would cross back over the Elbe, which they had crossed; they broke their Caudine Forks treaty as soon as they learned that we had been beaten at Rossbach. Indiscipline, desertion and illness destroyed our army, and the result of all our operations was that by the spring of 1758 we had lost three hundred millions, and fifty thousand men in Germany, fighting on behalf of Maria Theresa, just as we had done in the war of 1741 when we had fought against her.

The King of Prussia, who had beaten our army in Thuringia, at Rossbach, went off to fight against the Austrian army sixty leagues away from there. The French could have still entered Saxony, the victors were marching off elsewhere; nothing would have stopped the French; but they had thrown down their weapons, lost their cannon, their munitions, their food supplies, and above all their heads. They scattered. It was only with difficulty that their remnants could be reassembled. Exactly a month later, Frederick won a more signal and more precarious victory over the Austrian army, near Breslau; he recaptured Breslau, taking fifteen thousand prisoners; the rest of Silesia returned to his governance: Gustavus Adolphus had never accomplished such feats. So one had to forgive him his poetry, his jokes, his petty malice and even his sins against the female sex. All the failings of the man vanished before the fame of the hero.

At Les Délices, 6th November 1759

This was the point at which I had left my *Memoirs*, thinking them to be as pointless as Bayle's *Letters* to his dear mother, and the *Life of Saint-Evremond* written by Des Maiseaux, and that of the Abbé de Montgon written by himself;[60] but many of the things which seem to me either new or amusing remind me nonetheless of how ridiculous it is to talk about myself to myself.

From my windows I can see the city where Jean Chauvin of Picardy, known as Calvin, held his reign, and the square where he had Servetus burnt at stake for the good of his soul.[61] Almost all the priests in that city now think the same way as did Servetus, and go even further than he did. They do not at all believe that Jesus Christ was God; and those gentlemen, who in bygone days robbed purgatory of its souls, have become humane enough to show mercy to the souls in hell. They claim that their punishment will not be eternal, that Theseus will not always be confined to his seat, that Sisyphus will not always roll his stone:[62] thus they have turned hell, in which they no longer believe, into purgatory, in which they did not use to believe. This is quite a pretty little revolution in the history of the human mind. It provided pretext enough for a cutting of throats, lighting of pyres and general massacring *à la* St Bartholomew's Day;[63] and yet there was not even an exchange of insults, so changed are customs and manners. Only I was the recipient of such insults on the part of one of those preachers, because I had dared to suggest that the Picard Calvin had shown harshness of spirit by ill-advisedly burning Servetus. Wonder, if you please, at the contradictions of this world. Here are people who are almost all openly followers of Servetus, and yet insult me for having demurred at Calvin's having him slowly burned over bundles of fresh green firewood.

They wanted to prove to me definitively that Calvin was a good man; they requested that the Council of Geneva hand over the documents relating to the trial of Servetus: the Council, being wiser than they, refused; they were not permitted to write against me in Geneva. I regard this small triumph as the finest example of the progress made by reason this century.

Philosophy won an even greater victory over its enemies in Lausanne. Several ministers had taken it into their heads, in that country, to compile a nasty little book against me, for the honour, so they said, of the Christian religion. I managed without any difficulty to have the copies seized and suppressed by order of the magistrate: this was perhaps the first time that theologians had been forced to shut up and respect a philosopher. You cannot be surprised if I have a passionate love for this country. All you thinking beings – let me tell you that it is very agreeable to live in a republic to whose leaders you can say, 'Come and have dinner at my place tomorrow.' However, I still have not found myself entirely free; and what, to my mind, is worth dwelling on is this: in order to be perfectly free, I have purchased some land in France. There were two plots that suited me well, a league away from Geneva; they had formerly enjoyed all the privileges of that city. I have been fortunate enough to obtain from the King written permission allowing me to keep these privileges. In short, I have so arranged my destiny that I am now independent both in Switzerland, on the territory of Geneva, and in France.

I hear a lot of talk about freedom, but I do not think there has ever been an individual in Europe who has procured himself such freedom as mine. Anyone who wishes, or who can, will follow my example.

There was certainly no better way of spending my time than seeking this freedom and tranquillity far from Paris. At that time, people there were as foolish and fanatical over puerile quarrels as they had been during the Fronde; only civil war was missing.[64] But as Paris had neither a King of the Market, such as the Duc de Beaufort, nor a coadjutor giving his blessing with a dagger,[65] there were merely civilian squabbles. These had begun with bank notes for the other world, invented, as I have already said, by the Archbishop of Paris, Beaumont, a stubborn man, doing his best to do his worst out of an excess of zeal, a complete madman, a real saint in the style of Thomas of Canterbury. The quarrel arose over a position at the Hôpital to which the *Parlement* of Paris claimed it had the right to appoint, and which the Archbishop deemed was a sacred position that depended solely on the Church. The whole of Paris took sides; the little Jansenist and Molinist factions[66] did not spare each other; the King wanted to treat them the way one sometimes treats people fighting in the street – you throw buckets of water over them to break them up. He judged both parties to be in the wrong, as was only right; but they simply became more envenomed: he exiled the Archbishop, he exiled the *Parlement*; but a master should not dismiss his domestics unless he is sure he can find others to replace them; the court was finally obliged to bring back the *Parlement*, since a so-called royal chamber, composed of councillors of State and rapporteurs, and set up to deal with lawsuits, had not found any clients. The Parisians had taken it into their heads to bring cases only to that court of justice named a *Parlement*. So all of its members were recalled, and felt they had won a signal victory over the King. They paternally warned him, in one of their remonstrances, that he must not exile his *Parlement* ever again, given that, as they put it, 'this set a bad example'. They eventually made such a fuss that the King resolved to quash one of their chambers and to reform the others. Thereupon, all those gentlmen resigned, except for the Grand Chamber; there was a buzz of protest: in the Palais de Justice, they declaimed publicly against the King. Everyone was breathing fire, and unfortunately they inflamed the brain of a lackey called Damiens, who was often to be found in the main hall.[67] It was proven, at the trial of this fanatic of justice, that he had no intention of killing the King, but only of inflicting a gentle chastisement on him. There is no idea that does not sometimes pass through men's minds. This wretched fellow had been an usher at the Jesuit school where I have sometimes seen schoolboys lashing out with penknives, and their ushers returning the favour. So Damiens set off for Versailles with this intention, and wounded the King, in the midst of his guards and courtiers, with one of those little penknives used to sharpen quills.

In the first horror of this incident, people did not fail to accuse the Jesuits of being responsible – they were, it was said, in possession by ancient custom. I have read a letter from a certain Father Griffet, saying: 'This time it was not us; now it is the turn of those gentlemen.' It was of course for the Grand Provost of the Court to judge the assassin, since the crime had been committed in the precincts of the King's palace. The wretched man started by accusing seven members of the court of enquiry: all that was needed was to allow this accusation to stand, and execute the criminal; in this way the King would make the *Parlement* forever hateful, and would give himself an advantage over it as enduring as the monarchy itself. It is believed that M. d'Argenson persuaded the King to give his *Parlement* permission to judge the case: he got his just desserts, since a week later he was stripped of his possessions and exiled.

The King was so indulgent as to give hefty pensions to the councillors who examined Damiens' case, as if they had rendered some signal and difficult service. This action proved the final blow: it inspired the gentlemen of the court with added self-confidence; they felt themselves to be important personages, and their fantasies of representing the nation and being the guardians and tutors of kings awoke: once this episode had passed, and they had nothing further to do, they amused themselves by persecuting philosophers.

Omer Joly de Fleury, attorney general of the Paris *Parlement*, stood before the assembled chambers and made a display of the most complete triumph ever won by ignorance, bad faith and hypocrisy.[68] Several writers, worthy of high esteem by their knowledge and their conduct, had come together to compose an immense dictionary of everything capable of enlightening the human mind;[69] this was a highly significant commercial venture for the booksellers of France: the Chancellor and the ministers encouraged such a fine enterprise. Already seven volumes had come out; they were being translated into Italian, English, German and Dutch; and this treasure, made available to every nation by the French, could be regarded as our greatest honour, for the excellent articles in the *Encyclopedic Dictionary* completely redeemed the bad ones (though there are rather a lot of these). The only criticism that could be made of this work was the excessive number of puerile declamations, unfortunately adopted by the authors of the collection, who drew on all kinds of second-hand work to pad out the volume – but everything written by the authors themselves is excellent.

Along came Omer Joly de Fleury. On 23rd February 1759 he accused these poor men of being atheists, deists, corruptors of youth, rebels to the King, etc. To prove these accusations, Omer quoted Saint Paul, the trial of Théophile[70] and Abraham Chaumeix.* The only thing he had not done was to actually read the book he was denouncing – or, if he *had* read it, Omer was a total imbecile. He asked for the court to condemn the article *Soul*, which, in his view, promoted the purest materialism. You will notice that this article *Soul*, one of the worst in the whole book, is the work of a poor doctor of the Sorbonne who flogs himself to death by declaiming left, right and centre against materialism.[71] Omer Joly de Fleury's whole speech was a tissue of similar gross misreadings. Thus it was that he brought to justice the book that he had not read (or that he had not understood); and the whole *Parlement*, at Omer's demand, condemned the work, not only without even giving

* Abraham Chaumeix, previously a vinegar maker, had become a Jansenist and convulsionary: he was at this time the oracle of the *Parlement* of Paris. Omer Fleury quoted him as a Father of the Church. Chaumeix later became a schoolmaster in Moscow. (*Voltaire's note*)

it a fair trial, but without even reading a single page of it. This way of administering justice is far inferior to that of Bridoye, since at least Bridoye's decisions were occasionally correct.[72]

The publishers had been given the King's permission to print the work. *Parlement* certainly has no right to overturn permission granted by His Majesty; it is not competent to judge either a decree of the Council or anything that is signed and sealed in the Chancellery: nonetheless, it arrogated to itself the right to condemn all that the Chancellor had approved; it appointed councillors to decide on the information on geometry and metaphysics contained in the *Encyclopédie*. A Chancellor with any firmness of character would have quashed the decree of the *Parlement* as being inadmissible: the Chancellor, de Lamoignon, contented himself with re-voking the royal permission, so he would not have to endure the shame of seeing judged and condemned something on which he had bestowed the seal of the supreme authority. You would have thought that this train of events belonged to the time of Père Garasse and the decrees against the use of emetics;[73] and yet it occurred in the only enlightened century that France has ever enjoyed. Thus it is that a single fool can dishonour a whole nation. One can easily conclude that, in circumstances such as these, Paris was not a worthy dwelling place for a philosopher, and that Aristotle was very wise to retire to Chalcis when fanaticism was gaining the upper hand in Athens.[74] In any case, the status of a writer in Paris is only slightly higher than that of a street entertainer: the status of a gentleman ordinary of His Majesty, which the King had allowed me to keep, is not particularly elevated. Men are fools, and I think it is better to build a fine château, as I have done, and to put on plays there and enjoy a well-stocked table, rather than be hunted down like Helvétius, by the people who stand around in the courtyard of *Parlement* and the people who stand around in the stables of the Sorbonne.[75] Since I was sure I could not make men more reasonable, nor *Parlement* less pedantic, nor theologians less ridiculous, I continued to enjoy my happiness far from them.

I am almost ashamed of this happiness when, from my harbour, I gaze out at all the storms: I see Germany drenched with blood, France ruined from top to bottom, our armies and our fleets beaten, our ministers dismissed one after the other, without our affairs flourishing any better for it; the King of Portugal has been assassinated, not by a lackey, but by the nobles of his country, and this time the Jesuits cannot say: *It was not us.* They had held onto their rights, and it has been definitively proved since then that the Reverend Fathers had reverently placed the knives into the hands of the parricides. They say in justification that they are sovereigns in Paraguay, and that they have treated with the King of Portugal as one kingly power to another.[76]

And here is a little turn of events as singular as any that has been seen since there have been kings and poets on earth: Frederick, after spending quite a while guarding the frontiers of Silesia in an impregnable camp, grew bored there, and, to pass the time, he wrote an ode against France and its king. At the beginning of May 1759, he sent me his ode, signed 'Frederick', and accompanied by a huge parcel of poetry and prose. I opened the parcel, and saw that I was not the first to have opened it: it was evident that it had been unsealed en route. I froze with horror when I read the following stanzas of the ode:

> *Luxembourg and old Turenne*
> *Led warriors bold to glory;* [77]

They risked life and limb
As they fought for victory.
But now, oh vain and idle nation,
Your soldiers show their valour
In pillaging and plunder;
Real battle fills them with such consternation
They quickly turn and flee.

Your weak and feeble King,
La Pompadour's plaything,
Marked by the scars of love,
Too lazy even to move,
Hands o'er the reins to chance
And will not save his country, France
That's threatened with disaster;
He's just a slave pretending to be master.
He lies at ease under a beech-wood tree
And dares to boss around real kings like me!

Yes, I trembled when I saw this poem; there are some very good lines in it, or at least some lines that could pass as such. 'Unfortunately,' I thought, 'I have the well-deserved reputation of having hitherto corrected the poetry of the King of Prussia. The parcel has been opened en route, the poetry will be made public, the King of France will think that I wrote it, and I will be considered to have committed high treason, and, what is worse, of offending Madame de Pompadour.'

In this perplexity, I asked the resident of France in Geneva to come and see me; I showed him the parcel; he agreed that it must have been unsealed before reaching me. He decided that the only thing to be done, in a case where I risked being deprived of my head, was to send the parcel to M. le Duc de

Choiseul, the minister in France:[78] in any other circumstance I would not have taken this step; but I was obliged to forestall my ruin: I revealed to the Court the depths of its enemy's character. I knew that the Duc de Choiseul would not abuse this information, and that he would remain content with persuading the King of France that the King of Prussia was an irreconcilable enemy who had to be crushed, if possible. The Duc de Choiseul was not content to leave things there; he is a man of great intelligence, he writes poetry, he has friends who do so as well; he paid the King of Prussia back in his own coin, and sent me an ode against Frederick, as mordant and terrible as Frederick's against us had been. Here are some specimen passages:

In your halls, the lamp of learning,
Germany, now no more is burning.
That genius who once the arts did favour
Has failed as monarch, husband, son and brother.
His father had a most inspired idea
When once he tried his infant son to smother.

And yet this is the man who has the gall
To think himself the god of Thrace,[79] and all
Nine Muses in one single man combined.
In fact, at Mars's table, as on Parnassus
His place is much more modest: he's confined
Between the critics, Zoilus and Maevius.[80]

Despite his Roman guards, he's just a Nero
Chased out onto the stage to play a Pierrot –
The object of the scorn of all his legions.
We see the cruel King of Syracuse

Condemned to prostitute his sterile Muse
To all the jeers and insults of the nations.

So do not show such disrespect for others,
And be less carping when it comes to lovers
Who share in all love's pure and natural joys.
How dare you mock at love, when you have never
Experienced its ecstasy, fret and fever,
But in the arms of little drummer-boys?

When the Duc de Choiseul sent me this response, he assured me that he would have it printed if the King of Prussia published his work, and that Frederick would be beaten by the might of the pen just as decisively as we hoped to beat him by the might of the sword. If I had been after a little amusement, here was my chance: I could have looked on as the King of France and the King of Prussia waged poetic war on one another: this was a sight never before seen in the world. I gave myself another pleasure instead: that of being more sensible than Frederick. I wrote to tell him that his ode was a fine one, but that he ought not to make it public, that he did not need the fame, and that he ought not to close off every road to reconciliation with the King of France, to anger him irretrievably and force him to do all in his power to exact vengeance. I added that my niece had burned his ode, being mortally afraid that it might be attributed to me. He believed me, and thanked me, though not without rebuking me for burning the best poetry he had ever written in his life. The Duc de Choiseul, for his part, kept his word and was discreet.

To bring the joke to a fitting conclusion, I devised the plan of laying the first foundations of a European peace on these two documents that risked perpetuating war until Frederick was crushed. My correspondence with the Duc de Choiseul gave me this idea; it struck me as so ridiculous, so worthy of everything then happening, that I embraced it; and I gave myself the satisfaction of proving by myself how small and fragile are the pivots on which the destinies of kingdoms turn. Monsieur de Choiseul wrote me several open letters, couched in such a way that the King of Prussia might hazard a few overtures for peace without Austria taking umbrage at the ministry of France; and Frederick wrote me similar letters in which he did not risk displeasing the Court of London. This highly delicate correspondence is still ongoing; it resembles the expressions on the faces of two cats as they show, on the one side, a velvet glove and, on the other, claws unsheathed. The King of Prussia, beaten by the Russians, has lost Dresden, and needs peace; and France, beaten on land by the Hanoverians, and at sea by the English, has wasted its money to no purpose and is being forced to bring an end to this ruinous war.

This, my lovely Emilie, is the point we have reached.[81]

At Les Délices, this 27th November 1759

I will continue: there are still strange things to relate. The King of Prussia wrote to me on 17th December: 'I will write in more detail from Dresden, where I will be in three days'; and on the third day he was beaten by Maréchal Daun, and lost eighteen thousand men. It seems to me that everything I see is the fable of the *Milk Jug*.[82] Our great sailor Berryer, who was previously lieutenant of police in Paris, and who moved from that position to being Secretary of State and Naval Minister (even though he had never seen any fleet other than the canal barge of Saint-

Cloud or the passenger barge at Auxerre) – well, this Berryer of ours had taken it into his head to man a good number of ships and land on the coast of England: hardly had our fleet put its nose out of Brest than it was beaten by the English, broken up on the rocks, destroyed by the winds or swallowed up in the sea.

The man appointed to be our Controller General of Finances was a certain Silhouette whom we knew only as the man who had translated into prose some of the poetry of Pope:[83] he had the reputation of an eagle; but in less than four months the eagle was transformed into a gosling. He found a way of abolishing credit, with the result that the State suddenly found itself without any money to pay its troops. The King was obliged to send his entire dinner service to the Mint; a large number of people in the kingdom followed his example.

12th February 1760

Finally, after a few perfidious actions on the part of the King of Prussia, such as sending to London letters with which I had entrusted him, trying to sow discord between us and our allies (all of which are perfidious actions which are entirely permissible in a great king, especially in time of war), I have received peace proposals from the King of Prussia, with some poetry attached; he just cannot help writing it. I have forwarded the proposals to Versailles; I am doubtful that they will be accepted: he refuses to surrender any land, and suggests, to indemnify the Elector of Saxony, that he be given Erfurt, which belongs to the Elector of Mainz: he always has to deprive someone of something; that is the kind of man he is. We will see what results from these ideas and especially from the campaign upon which they are about to embark.

As this great and terrible tragedy is never without its comic side, they have just published in Paris the *Pohetry of the King my master*, as Freytag used to call it; there is an epistle to Marischal Keith, in which he makes great fun of the immortality of the soul and mocks the Christians. The *dévots* are not pleased, the Calvinist priests are grumbling; these pedants regarded him as being on the right side, they admired him when he flung the magistrates of Leipzig into the dungeons, and sold their cushy jobs to get his hands on their money. But ever since he has seen fit to translate a few passages of Seneca, Lucretius and Cicero, they regard him as a monster. If Cartouche had been a *dévot*, the priests would have canonised him.[84]

NOTES

1. Emilie du Châtelet (1706–49) was an outstanding scientist and mathematician. Unusually well-educated for a woman of the time, she became fluent in Greek and Latin, German and Italian. Her marriage was an arranged one: it produced three children, whereupon she and her husband agreed to lead separate lives. She had an affair with the Duc de Richelieu, who encouraged her interest in mathematics: she took geometry lessons from Maupertuis, who was an expert on the theories of Newton. She invited Voltaire to live with her at her country house in Cirey (Haute-Marne); he was thirty-nine at the time, she was twenty-seven; they embarked on an affair, and several years of shared intellectual endeavours ensued. Madame du Châtelet produced highly original studies on the nature of fire and light, matter and movement: her most celebrated work, completed in the year she died, was her translation of Newton's *Principia*, with commentary.

2. Anne Dacier (1647–1720) was a philologist and classicist. She translated several Greek and Latin authors including the Latin comic writers Terence and Plautus.

3. Samuel König (1712–57) was a German mathematician.

4. Pierre Louis Maupertuis (1698–1759) was a French mathematician: he supported Newton against the Cartesians. He was already a member of the French *Académie des Sciences* by the time he was twenty-five. He was invited to Berlin at the invitation of Frederick, and took part in the battle of Mollwitz, as Voltaire goes on to relate below. He returned to Paris and then went back to Berlin, where in 1746 he was made president of the Prussian Royal Academy of Sciences.

5. Jean (or Johann) Bernoulli (1647–1748) was a Swiss mathematician. His jealousy and his tendency to appropriate ideas from others were noted by many people as well as Voltaire.

6. Francesco Algarotti (1712–64) was an Italian art connoisseur of wide general knowledge who was acquainted with many of the leading figures of the Enlightenment. His book *Newtonianism for Ladies* (1737) was one of the main attempts to popularise the new scientific ideas.

7. This book (roughly, 'Lessons in Physics') was written for Mme du Châtelet's thirteen-year-old son; published in 1740, it contained some highly advanced ideas on mass and momentum.

8. Alexis Clairaut (1713–65), a brilliant French mathematician who specialised in geodesy.

9. These were all plays by Voltaire.

10. Jacques Bénigne Bossuet (1627–1704), Bishop of Meaux, the great French preacher and author of the *Discours sur l'histoire universelle* (1681), a planned history of the world, which was left unfinished. The completed sections focused on Old Testament history and did not get beyond Charlemagne.

11. Johan de Witt (1625–72) was Grand Pensionary of the States of Holland. He ruled the Dutch Republic for much of its Golden Age, but his pro-French policies led to his downfall when France joined forces with England to attack the Dutch Republic in 1672; ousted by supporters of the House of Orange, he and his brother Cornelis were murdered by a lynch mob.

12. Frederick William I of Prussia (1688–1740), of the House of Hohenzollern, the 'Soldier King', was the father of Frederick William II, 'the Great' (1712–86).

13. This special regiment of very tall men, recruited from all over Europe, was known as the 'lange Kerls' ('lanky fellows') or the Potsdam Giants.

14. Heyducks were originally mercenary foot soldiers in Hungary, but the word was later used to refer to attendants in German or Hungarian courts.

15. Hans Hermann von Katte (1704–30) was a close friend (some say lover) of Frederick the Great when the latter was still only a prince. Peter Karl Christoph Keith (1711–56) was also very close to Frederick, and acted as his page.

16. Her name was Doris Ritter; she was imprisoned in Spandau jail until 1733.

17. In 1718, Alexei Petrovich, son of Tsar Peter I ('the Great') died under sentence of death, after considerable ill treatment from his father, who accused him of treason.

18. Christian Wolff (1679–1754) was a German philosopher of the Enlightenment.

19. These were both seventeenth-century French poets.

20. Lucius Licinius Lucullus (*c*.118–56 BC) was a Roman consul who retired from politics to enjoy a life of leisure and luxury.

21. The Abbé Pierre François Guyot-Desfontaines (1685–1745) was a journalist and literary critic, and a noted enemy of Voltaire, even though the latter had intervened to save him from the potentially capital charge of sodomy.

22. Emperor Charles VI, Holy Roman Emperor, died in 1740.

23. André-Hercule, Cardinal de Fleury (1653–1743) was chief minister of Louis XV. He helped France recover from the crisis provoked by the collapse of Law's bank (see note 48 below), partly by extorting forced labour from the peasants.

24. As well as being King of Prussia, Frederick was also the Elector of Brandenburg, i.e. he was one of the eight dignitaries who elected the Holy Roman Emperor.

25. The battle of Mollwitz was fought on 10th April 1741. The Prussians won despite losing more men (some 3,900 dead or wounded) than the Austrians (2,500 dead or wounded). Frederick had started the war (The War of the Austrian Succession, 1740–48) by invading Silesia in December 1740.

26. The *dévots* ('devout') were a recognisable camp in French intellectual life: strict Catholics of avowedly austere morals, who during the eighteenth century opposed the Enlightenment.

27. This 1738 work by Voltaire was an important milestone in the introduction of Newton's philosophy into France.

28. The 'St Thomas' here is Aquinas. Pasquier Quesnel (1634–1719) was a theologian who belonged to the Jansenist wing of the Catholic Church (persuaded that human beings could contribute nothing to their salvation without divine grace).

29. The Pragmatic Sanction of 1713 ensured that the throne of the Holy Roman Emperor would go to the daughter of Charles VI, Maria Theresa. When Charles died in 1740, however, some of the signatories (France, Bavaria, Prussia and Saxony) refused to accept her accession: this led to the War of the Austrian Succession.

30. The Theatines, a male religious order in the Catholic Church, were founded in 1524.

31. The words *anc.* (for *ancien*) *évêque de Mirepoix*, mean 'former Bishop of Mirepoix'; *l'âne de Mirepoix* means 'the donkey (of) Mirepoix'.

32. Epaminondas, the Theban general (d. 362 BC), was (like the abovementioned Marcus Aurelius, the Stoic Roman emperor) a man of somewhat austere tastes. Unlike Marcus Aurelius, he was not an intellectual, though he was admired by intellectuals (Cicero, Montaigne).

33. Encolpius is the protagonist of the Latin satirical novel the *Satyricon* by Petronius Arbiter. Giton is his sixteen-year-old boyfriend.

34. The word abbreviated (in French as *v...*) is no doubt *vit*, 'prick'.

35. Jean-Baptiste de Boyer, Marquis d'Argens (1704–71) was a nobleman who helped to spread Enlightenment ideas: he was summoned by Frederick to Potsdam, but later offended him by marrying a Berlin actress, Mlle Cochois. Baron Karl Ludwig Pöllnitz (1692–1775), after a youth spent as a soldier of adventure, became the first chamberlain of Frederick's court and a favourite of the King.

36. Pierre Bayle (1647–1706) was one of Voltaire's favourite modern philosophers. His *Historical and Critical Dictionary* (1697) was a work of labyrinthine cross-referencing and footnotes to footnotes, whose sceptical attitudes had a profound influence on the Enlightenment.

37. Louis XII became King of France in 1498; in the preceding war between rival French factions, while still Duc d'Orléans, he had spent considerable time in various French prisons. He adopted a conciliatory approach on his accession.

38. Pietro Metastasio (1698–1782) was the celebrated librettist whose words for *La Clemenza di Tito* were set by nearly forty composers, and an edited version of his text was the basis for Mozart's last opera of the same name (1791).

39. Jeanne-Antoinette Poisson (1721–64) became Mme Le Normant d'Etiolles and then, in 1745, the King's mistress; she was given the title Mme de Pompadour.

40. Stanislas I (1677–1766) was King of Poland during two periods, but abdicated in 1736 and was created Duke of Lorraine and Bar; he settled in Lunéville and devoted himself to intellectual pursuits.

41. Christophe de Beaumont (1703–81), Archbishop of Paris at this time, was a fierce persecutor of the Jansenists, the austere Augustinian wing of the Catholic Church. He ordered the priests in his diocese to refuse a religious burial to anyone who had made confession to a Jansenist priest.

42. Astolfo is a knight errant in Ariosto's *Orlando Furioso*, and like many others he is smitten by the charms of the enchantress Alcina, to whom Voltaire a little snidely compares Frederick.

43. Julian Offray de La Mettrie (1709–51) was a materialist philosopher whose main work, *L'Homme machine*, depicts human beings as complex mechanisms.

44. Dionysius I of Syracuse (*c*. 432–367 BC) was a cruel tyrant, a poet and a patron of literature. His son Dionysius II (*c*. 397–343 BC) was unsuccessfully tutored for a while by Plato.

45. Maupertuis wrote a 'Letter on Scientific Progress' indicating the direction future research should take. Voltaire here parodies the ideas contained in it, though in some cases he does not exaggerate very much (Maupertuis did indeed advocate dissecting the brains of the giants said to live in Patagonia). Maupertuis had already been, if not to the poles, at least on an expedition to Lapland, in 1736, to measure one degree of the earth's meridian there. It turned out to be longer than in France, and this supported Newton's theory that the earth was slightly flat at the poles. Frederick, angered at the slight to the Berlin Academy he detected in Voltaire's scorn, defended Maupertuis – hence the final souring of relations between them.

46. Samuel König visited Berlin in 1750 and pointed out numerous errors in an *Essay on Cosmology* published by Maupertuis. König claimed to have a letter by Leibniz establishing a 'principle of least action' in physics before Maupertuis; the latter, piqued at having the priority of his discovery taken from him, persuaded the Berlin Academy to declare that this letter was a forgery.

47. Voltaire ironically plays, as so often, with the titles of the royal figures involved in these dynastic squabbles: the Margrave of Brandenburg was Frederick.

48. Pierre Guérin de Tencin (1679–1758) was Archbishop of Embrun and Lyons; in 1742, Louis XV made him a minister without portfolio. John Law (1671–1729), the Scottish economist, was appointed Controller General of Finances, and set up a national bank in France, but this eventually collapsed, leading to a major financial crisis across Europe.

49. *Le Mondain* or *The Man of the World* was a poem by Voltaire that attacked the Jansenist contempt for this world.

50. Voltaire is here describing the outbreak of the Seven Years War (1756–63), which – given that so many of Europe's far-flung colonies were also involved – is sometimes considered to be the first real 'world war'.

51. Veteravia (modern Wetterau) is a region in Hesse, Germany.

52. This was the battle of Kolín (18th June 1757), to the east of Prague. The Prussians lost some 14,000 men, the Austrians about 9,000: it was Frederick's first defeat in the Seven Years War.

53. At the Battle of the Caudine Forks (321 BC), the Roman army found itself trapped in a narrow defile: forced to surrender, its soldiers were humiliated by being made to pass under a yoke, i.e. they were *subjugated*.

54. The 'Imperial circles' (*Reichskreise*) were ten regional groupings of the states of the Holy Roman Empire.

55. Philomel, here short for Philomela, who was raped by Tereus; he cut out her tongue to prevent her telling of his crime; she was eventually turned into a nightingale.

56. Cato and Brutus are here dragooned into service by Frederick as stoical suicides.

57. Prometheus was not exactly condemned to hell, but to a rock in the Caucasus, where an eagle constantly devoured his liver.

58. Ixion was bound to a spinning fiery wheel for having lusted after Hera.

59. William Augustus, the Duke of Cumberland, was known as 'Butcher' Cumberland for his part in crushing the Jacobites after Culloden in 1746. His later military career was less brilliant; during the Seven Years War he was sent to the continent to protect British interests (Hanover) in alliance with Frederick, but after being defeated by d'Estrées he capitulated to the Duc de Richelieu and withdrew from the war in 1757. It is presumably this latter action, rather than his treatment of the Highlanders, that Voltaire is here recommending to Frederick.

60. These are all given as examples of works that were too radical to be published with impunity.

61. Michael Servetus (1511–53) was a Spanish theologian whose rejection of the doctrine of the Trinity (i.e. his denial of the divinity of Christ) alienated him from both Protestants and Catholics. His rejection of predestination to hell angered Calvin, and he was burned at the stake outside Geneva.

62. Theseus was trapped by Hades, who invited him to a feast in the underworld; when Theseus sat in his chair, snakes coiled round his legs, and the stone of the chair bound him to it. He was, however, eventually rescued by Heracles. Sisyphus was condemned to roll a stone uphill for all eternity, since it was forever rolling back downhill again.

63. St Bartholomew's Day, 24th August 1572 marked the start of months of Catholic violence against the Protestants in France.

64. The Fronde (1648–53) was a civil war in France.

65. The Duc de Beaufort (1616–69) was a popular figure in Paris during the Fronde. The Parisians named him 'Roi des Halles' ('King of the Market'). The coadjutor of Paris took a dagger in his pocket when he went into the *Parlement*.

66. Jansenists (strict predestinarians) versus Molinists (who inclined to the belief that humans can alter their eternal destiny by free will) was an ongoing ideological struggle in the eighteenth-century French Church.

67. Robert-François Damiens (1715–54) was a soldier and servant; he became obsessed by the idea that murdering King Louis XV would restore peace during the religious unrest attending, among other things, the persecution of the Jansenists. His attempt failed, but he was executed (drawn and quartered) on the Place de Grève in Paris. His gruesome execution is described at the beginning of Foucault's *Discipline and Punish*. Barbaric judicial executions of this kind were increasingly to prove the focus of Voltaire's polemics after the period narrated by the *Memoirs*.

68. Joseph Omer Joly de Fleury (1715–1810) was the butt of Voltaire's satire because in 1763 he temporarily forbade inoculation, a practice which was becoming increasingly common; he also condemned Helvétius' work *De l'Esprit* and the *Encyclopédie*.

69. The *Encyclopédie* (the great *Encyclopedia or Analytical Dictionary of the Sciences, Arts, and Trades*), edited by Diderot and D'Alembert and published between 1751 and 1772, was a colossal undertaking that, with its focus on technological progress, its system of subversive cross-referencing, and (in the best articles) its irony and stylishness, celebrated the new sciences and fostered a critical attitude towards inherited (especially theological) wisdom. Voltaire contributed several articles, including those on 'Fire', 'Faith', and 'Fornication'.

70. Théophile de Viau (1590–1626), a libertine poet, denounced by the Jesuits and condemned to be burnt alive (1623) eventually had his sentence commuted to banishment for life. His trial divided contemporary intellectual opinion.

71. There are in fact three articles on 'Soul' in the *Encyclopédie,* two by the Abbé Yvon, and one by Diderot.

72. Bridoie is a lawyer in Rabelais who reaches his decisions by a throw of the dice.

73. François Garasse (1585–1631) was a Jesuit and a particularly fanatical preacher against the University of Paris.

74. Aristotle left Athens for Chalcis in Euboea to avoid the fate of Socrates; he had been the tutor of the Macedonian Alexander the Great, on whose death the Athenians rose against Macedonian hegemony.

75. Claude Adrien Helvétius (1715–71) was a French *philosophe* whose *De L'Esprit* (*On the Mind*), published in 1758, was burnt as atheistic. He went to Berlin in 1765 at the invitation of Frederick.

76. An attempt on the life of Joseph I of Portugal was made by a group of nobles in 1758; it was alleged that the Jesuits had foreknowledge of the attempt (which the King – who, incidentally, had suffered from claustrophobia ever since the Lisbon earthquake of 1755 recorded in *Candide* – survived).

77. The Duc de Luxembourg and the Vicomte de Turenne were celebrated seventeenth-century French generals.

78. Etienne-François, Duc de Choiseul (1719–85) was a statesman who was generally quite well thought of by the *philosophes*; he allowed the *Encyclopédie* to be published.

79. The 'God of Thrace' is Dionysus.

80. The Greek Zoilus and Roman Maevius were both carping critics from classical times.

81. This is a quotation from Corneille's play *Cinna* (1640) in which the heroine, Emilie, spurs on her lover, Cinna, to kill the Roman Emperor Octavian (Augustus). When the plot fails, the emperor pardons them. The fact that Mme du Châtelet's first name had been Emilie, and the regicidal theme (given the context of Voltaire's disaffection with Frederick) may be of significance.

82. In the fable of the *Pot au lait* (La Fontaine, *Fables*, VII, 9), the milkmaid is going off to market, dreaming of all the wealth the jug of milk she is carrying will bring her. She trips and spills it all.

83. Etienne de Silhouette (1709–67) was the Finance Minister under Louis XV. As well as being a translator, he faced economic crisis by taxing the wealthy middle classes in 1759 and ordering gold and silver to be melted down to help finance the Seven Years War. The word 'silhouette' is derived from his name, either because the victims of his taxation complained that he reduced them to mere outlines, or because he enjoyed cutting shapes out of paper in his retirement.

84. Louis Dominique Bourguignon, known as Cartouche, was a celebrated French highwayman (1693–1721) who was eventually broken on the wheel.

BIOGRAPHICAL NOTE

François-Marie Arouet, better known by his pen name Voltaire, was born into a middle-class family in Paris in 1694. He was educated by the Jesuits at the Collège Louis-le-Grand, where he learnt Latin and Greek. He went on to study law before devoting himself entirely to writing.

An outspoken critic of the French government and the Catholic church, Voltaire was often in trouble with the French authorities. He was committed to the Bastille from 1717–18 and exiled to England in 1726, where he stayed for three years. He then returned to Paris, and published a collection of essays, *Philosophical Letters on the English* (1734), extolling England's constitutional monarchy and religious tolerance. These were met with controversy in Paris, with copies being burnt, and Voltaire was forced to leave the capital.

From Paris, Voltaire went to the Château de Cirey in the Haute-Marne region, where he formed a close relationship with the Marquise du Châtelet, a mathematician and scientist who was extremely well educated for a woman of her time. Together, they undertook numerous experiments and intellectual endeavours over a period of fifteen years, until the Marquise died in 1749.

Voltaire then moved to Berlin at the invitation of King Frederick the Great where he was, for a while, very happy. However, he later fell out with Maupertuis, the President of the Berlin Academy of Science, and mocked him in *The Diatribe of Doctor Akakia* (1753), which caused the King to order his arrest. Voltaire was obliged to move again, this time to Ferney, near Geneva in Switzerland, where he finally settled for almost all of the last twenty years of his life. It was here he wrote the work for which he is best known, the satirical novel *Candide* (1759).

Voltaire died in Paris in 1778 and is buried in the Panthéon.

Andrew Brown studied at the University of Cambridge, where he taught French for many years. He now works as a freelance teacher and translator. He is the author of *Roland Barthes: The Figures of Writing* (OUP, 1993), and his translations include *Memoirs of a Madman* by Gustave Flaubert, *For A Night of Love* by Emile Zola, *The Jinx* by Théophile Gautier, *Mademoiselle de Scudéri* by E.T.A. Hoffman, *Theseus* by André Gide, *Incest* by Marquis de Sade, *Colonel Chabert* by Honoré de Balzac, *Memoirs of an Egotist* by Stendhal, *Butterball* by Guy de Maupassant, *With the Flow* by Joris-Karl Huysmans and *Journey to the Moon* by Cyrano de Bergerac, all published by Hesperus Press.

HESPERUS PRESS CLASSICS

Hesperus Press, as suggested by the Latin motto, is committed to bringing near what is far – far both in space and time. Works written by the greatest authors, and unjustly neglected or simply little known in the English-speaking world, are made accessible through new translations and a completely fresh editorial approach. Through these classic works, the reader is introduced to the greatest writers from all times and all cultures.

For more information on Hesperus Press, please visit our website: **www.hesperuspress.com**

ET REMOTISSIMA PROPE

SELECTED TITLES FROM HESPERUS PRESS

Author	Title	Foreword writer
Pietro Aretino	*The School of Whoredom*	Paul Bailey
Pietro Aretino	*The Secret Life of Nuns*	
Jane Austen	*Lesley Castle*	Zoë Heller
Jane Austen	*Love and Friendship*	Fay Weldon
Honoré de Balzac	*Colonel Chabert*	A.N. Wilson
Charles Baudelaire	*On Wine and Hashish*	Margaret Drabble
Giovanni Boccaccio	*Life of Dante*	A.N. Wilson
Charlotte Brontë	*The Spell*	
Emily Brontë	*Poems of Solitude*	Helen Dunmore
Mikhail Bulgakov	*Fatal Eggs*	Doris Lessing
Mikhail Bulgakov	*The Heart of a Dog*	A.S. Byatt
Giacomo Casanova	*The Duel*	Tim Parks
Miguel de Cervantes	*The Dialogue of the Dogs*	Ben Okri
Geoffrey Chaucer	*The Parliament of Birds*	
Anton Chekhov	*The Story of a Nobody*	Louis de Bernières
Anton Chekhov	*Three Years*	William Fiennes
Wilkie Collins	*The Frozen Deep*	
Joseph Conrad	*Heart of Darkness*	A.N. Wilson
Joseph Conrad	*The Return*	Colm Tóibín
Gabriele D'Annunzio	*The Book of the Virgins*	Tim Parks
Dante Alighieri	*The Divine Comedy: Inferno*	
Dante Alighieri	*New Life*	Louis de Bernières
Daniel Defoe	*The King of Pirates*	Peter Ackroyd
Marquis de Sade	*Incest*	Janet Street-Porter
Charles Dickens	*The Haunted House*	Peter Ackroyd
Charles Dickens	*A House to Let*	
Fyodor Dostoevsky	*The Double*	Jeremy Dyson
Fyodor Dostoevsky	*Poor People*	Charlotte Hobson
Alexandre Dumas	*One Thousand and One Ghosts*	